A Way To Escape 2

The journey of Rose, now an undocumented domestic worker in Canada, continues...

Michelle F. Thompson

LMH PUBLISHING LIMITED

© 2025 Michelle Thompson
First Edition
10 9 8 7 6 5 4 3 2 1

All rights reserved. No part of this book may be reproduced, stored in a retrieval system, or transmitted, in any form or by any means, electronic, mechanical, photocopying, recording, or otherwise, without the prior written permission of the publishers or author.

This is a work of fiction. Names, characters, places and incidents either are the products of the author's imagination or are used fictitiously, and any resemblance to actual persons, living or dead, events or locales, is entirely coincidental.

All LMH Publishing Limited titles are available at special quantity discounts for bulk purchases for sales promotion, premiums, fund-raising, educational or institutional use.

Editor: K. Sean Harris
Cover Design: Sanya Dockery
Book Design, Layout & Typesetting: Sanya Dockery

Published by LMH Publishing Limited
Suite 10-11, Sagicor Industrial Park
7 Norman Road
Kingston C.S.O., Jamaica
Tel.: (876) 938-0005; 938-0712
Fax: (876) 759-8752
Email: lmhbookpublishing@cwjamaica.com
Website: www.lmhpublishing.com

Printed in the U.S.A.   ISBN: 978-976-657-130-6

**CATALOGUING-IN-PUBLICATION DATA AT THE
NATIONAL LIBRARY OF JAMAICA**

CHAPTER One

In the summer of 1970, the Jamaican community along Eglinton Avenue at Oakwood was abuzz. Jamaicans away from home parlayed the Toronto west-end strip, keeping barbershops, patty shops, fish and produce shops, busy. Cardboard barrels, small and jumbo for packing foreign goods being shipped to families back home, lined these shop entrances. Beauty parlour windows displayed wigged mannequins in all shapes, textures and colours, drew passersby inside. Passing cars flew black, green and yellow Jamaican flags high, entertaining the neighbourhood with too loud drum and base beats, their drivers honking horns at "nice-looking ladies". Ladies like Rose, who was new to Toronto, and her friend Gurley, seasoned to the west-end community, were decked out in sleeveless summer dresses and matching sandals. Rose's shoulder-length hair bounced with each stride, the handy work of Gurley who required nothing less for parading the avenue.

Near the end of their stroll, the two friends bought a couple of lottery tickets at the corner store, for the million-dollar draw later that night. Giddy from the prospect of a winning ticket, and a dream of a mansion in the hills of St. Andrew, back home, they waltzed into Pepper Pot, the restaurant next door. The Jamaican-owned eatery was a social hub for Caribbean people, landed and undocumented, for the chance to "lime" or "catch up on yard".

As the women entered, the stringed bamboo partition at the doorway clapped noisily announcing their presence. Two men sitting at a table near the door with beer in hand, and two full bottles on the table, sat up tall at their passing, their backs as broad as their smiles. The forty-seat establishment was almost at full capacity. From the jukebox, Bob Marley chanted "lively up yourself" and the patrons swayed in their seats and pranced on the dance floor. Amid laughter and the pounding of dominoes, the 70s rhythm never sounded sweeter.

Gurley, the chubbier of the two women, noticed the men, around fortyish, their age, eyeing her and Rose. She swiftly sucked in her tummy, drew the belt tighter around her waist, and swiped the back of her wig, pressing it in place on her nape.

A vacant table was on the opposite side of the room. In clear view of the men, she elbowed Rose to follow her.

One of the waitresses came and took their order right away. Rose remembered their friend at home and said to Gurley, "You think we should take something home for Cynthia?"

Cynthia was the older friend of both Rose and Gurley. She owned the home where they stayed.

"No, she's not too keen on restaurant food, especially with her sugar."

The smooth, velvety voice of Dennis Brown, Jamaica's "crown prince" of reggae, played in the background. Gurley tapped Rose on the hand and waved at her, and they went on the dance floor, a small space beside the jukebox for dancing.

They danced facing each other until one of the men, wearing a floral shirt and a lasting grin, joined them. He brought his beer with him, slowly gyrating in front of Rose. His eyes trailed her long, brown legs from the end of her mini-dress down to her pink sandals. Rose kept spinning, staying close to Gurley, not making eye contact with him. As the waitress walked across the room with their oxtail dinner on a tray, Rose and Gurley followed her back to the table. She served their meals and left.

Rose's admirer met the waitress at the counter. He whispered to her as he took a piece of paper from his pocket and gave it to her. A call for a fourth player at the domino table got his attention and he went to fill that seat. "Don't forget to give her, you know," he told the waitress, as he walked away.

Moments later the waitress brought two beers and a message for Rose. Rose glanced at the paper and left it on the table.

Gurley leaned over and read the name and phone number on it, and encouraged Rose to put it in her purse. "You never know," she said, "it might come in handy", and she laughed. Rose gave her the eye and reluctantly dropped it in her shoulder purse. Gurley, not letting up, said, "Why don't you go over and thank Roy?"

Rose casually turned her head to look at Roy. "Please," she said, rolling her eyes at him guzzling down a beer.

"At least give him a wave."

"I'm not looking for a liquor-head man and he looks like he's in love with that beer," Rose said. She had spotted Roy when she entered the restaurant with a beer in his hand, that apparently he couldn't let go of and had brought to the dance floor. Rose had developed a laser eye for guzzlers from years spent with an alcoholic husband who had substituted beers for his rum and water to maintain his buzz.

Gurley urged Rose to be nice, and she glanced over at Roy, "Mr. Pretty-Shirt" as she referred to him, waiting with his big grin, and she barely cracked a smile.

Rose was visiting Toronto on a three-week visa; she had come that Thursday, two days prior. As she and Gurley ate, Gurley reminded her that she should "act friendly and less choosey", and maybe she would "get lucky". Gurley was forever mindful of opportunities for permanency in Canada, herself two years in the country without her landed papers, and she lived life expectantly.

"I'm not desperate, Gurley," Rose answered.

"I know, but it sure would be nice to start getting a little money in your pocket."

"Yeah, but that don't mean I should act as if I have no choice."

"You wait 'til them four children start phoning you with all sorts of demands," Gurley said. She raised her head from her food, still holding her fork, and latched eyes with Rose. "You have them to feed," she continued, "and whether you going back home or not, you will need money." Gurley felt compelled to tell Rose not to make her mistake. "Don't be like me, pass up plenty opportunities thinking something or somebody better was going to come along."

Gurley's words sunk in, and Rose stared quietly back at Gurley, wondering how she managed being on her own, when Gurley said, "I wish I had a little man to help me, so if you find one to marry you, grab the opportunity."

"But who said this man looking for anybody?" Rose told Gurley.

"You won't know if you keep saying no."

They finished their meal and sipped their beer in silence.

Roy watched Rose all through his domino game. He smiled at her when he slammed the domino on the table, winning the game. Rose barely noticed him.

A couple cozying up in the corner happily went over to the jukebox and filled it with coins for their selections of slow music. Once the romantic music started, Rose told Gurley she was ready to go home, mostly to avoid what she thought surely was going to happen: Roy coming to ask her for a dance.

Before leaving the restaurant, Rose and Gurley went to the restroom. They freshened up and satisfied with themselves, exited into an unusually quiet atmosphere. The music had stopped, and an ominous panicky sound replaced it. The women stood outside the restroom door, huddled beside each other, wondering what the matter was.

Standing as if frozen in place, the waitress that served them earlier, bumped into them at the door. Her slender body, stooped against the wall, moved quickly. Her eyes were wide open and filled with fright, she was as a toad trying to escape menacing, stone-throwing boys. Only in her case, it was menacing immigration officers.

Rose detected something afoot, and dread stirred within her.

The waitress glanced up at them and whispered, "Immigration."

Gurley audibly gasped and dropped to the floor, pulling Rose by the hand down to the floor with her. The young woman beckoned for the women to follow her.

Laying low on the floor, Gurley had a harder time rising for the dash out an incognito door that separated the restroom from the kitchen. Once on her feet, fear propelled her past Rose.

Rose, running out into the darkness, was overwhelmed by the suddenness of everything. She slowed down and fell behind.

Gurley noticed Rose had stalled and she slowed enough to grab her hand. Rose tripped and her sandals fell off.

"My shoes!" Rose cried out.

"Don't stop, man, just come!"

Rose pulled from Gurley. "No, I'm not leaving it," she said, and shoved her foot into the plastic slippers. The strap across the toes had burst and she hopped-skipped behind Gurley as they cut through the neighbourhood backstreets.

It wasn't until at the corner of Eglinton and Bathurst Streets, many blocks from Pepper Pot Restaurant that Rose and Gurley finally stopped, the waitress in tow. A bus pulled up as they reached the bus stop. They got on the bus and laughing nervously, counted their blessings for a lucky escape.

Only a few people were on the bus and most of them sat in the front. The women went to the back row, Gurley and Rose sandwiched the waitress. They introduced themselves and learned that the young woman was Yvonne.

Settling into their seats, Rose caught her breath and asked Yvonne, "So what really happened back at the restaurant?" Rose was trying to understand how a joyous, carefree occasion ended with them running through the neighbourhood like disbanded thieves.

Yvonne closed her eyes and breathed in and out. She began, "It just happened so fast", she turned from one woman's gaze to the next and shook her head, coming to terms with the close call. "I was wiping down the counter and heard the partition clapped together like somebody walked in. I didn't look up at first, thinking nothing of it", she waved her hand, "as people come and go every minute." She ran her hand over the corners of her mouth and continued. "Then I heard a male voice, Canadian accent, say, 'good evening everyone' and that's when I looked up and saw the two of them." By now her eyes were watered and she squeezed them to stop the tears from flowing. She wiped her moist fingers in her skirt and shrugged. Straightening her shoulders, Yvonne paused to quickly run through her mind the last eight months of living in Toronto, and her plan to leave the country which she had been devising since her first month in Canada. She muttered, "Immigration can't stop me", with a certainty that hardened her face.

"How you sure it was immigration and not police?" Rose asked, her brows narrowed, her eyes searching Yvonne's.

Yvonne pulled back and said, "Because they had on their khaki uniform." She wasn't aware that Rose, new to Canada, wouldn't have known.

Gurley butted in. "Yes, I can tell them anywhere in that khaki uniform, although, it's not all of them wear uniform."

Rose looked off, imagining the khaki wearing men walking in and surprising the patrons.

"The older one," Yvonne continued, "immediately asked everybody for ID." She turned from Rose to Gurley, then back to Rose. "I duck down quick behind the counter and crawl to the back."

"Duck yes," Gurley said with a chuckle, before carrying on, "because when I see them on the street, I just turn 'round and go the other way or cross the street." She frowned, remembering the last time she had to walk a couple of blocks out of her way to avoid one of them.

Rose nodded slowly, taking in Yvonne and Gurley's immigration encounters, wondering if this too would be her path. An instant playback of the last hour confirmed it already was.

"Lord!" Yvonne yelled, and threw her hands up in the air, drawing attention back to her. Rose and Gurley stared at her. "Would you believe, me was so frightened that me run leave my handbag?" A loud, undeliberate sound left her throat, and she covered her face to keep from crying. When she removed her hands, her countenance changed. Her sadness switched to calm determination. "But I don't even care," she said. "Just as long as them never catch me", her voice grew softer, a little hoarse, "for I couldn't afford that right now." Her eyes narrowed then widened, as a thought popped into her mind. She quickly looked at both hips and patted her pants pockets, taking out bills of ones, twos and fives she'd made in tips. Arranging the bills heads up, she counted the money. "I'm saving every cent I have to go across the States." Folding the bills and putting them back into one pocket, she lowered her head, and whispered that her goal was to join her son's father in New York. "He was in Canada and somebody help him slip cross the border." Raising her head and her chin, she added, "And they going help me go over, too." Joy watered Yvonne's eyes.

Rose's mouth fell open as she penetrated Yvonne with awe, thinking if she were as brave as her, she would have been in Canada with landed status from the first time her friend Cynthia had mentioned for her to come. "Boy, you're daring though, very bold," she said, measuring the young woman's courage against her own. "And just from that one experience I had tonight, I don't know if I can do all this running, no man." She pursed her lips and shook her head.

"We do what we have to do, not what we always like. Because at the end of the day, it's all about survival. Nobody not going to give you anything in this country, you have to look it for yourself," Gurley answered, and resting her elbows on her knees, she cupped the solemn look on her face with both hands.

"Everybody has family to take care of back home, their pickney to feed," Yvonne added. "I had to leave my little four-year-old son with my mother. I never like it," she said, as Rose nodded, "but that's what I had to do if I wanted to make a better life for him. And when I get settled, I going bring him up, him and my mother."

Rose blinked, breaking from Yvonne's stare, and gazing down at her feet, noticed that the strap on her sandal was dangling. In scrutinizing the shoe, she saw that the stylishly

criss-cross straps at her toes were worn out, much like how she felt in that moment. Dejected, she let out a long sigh, shrugged off hopelessness and turned back to the conversation around her. The difference she realized then, with her and Yvonne's story, was that she had left four children back home, with no man waiting for them to be together again to raise their children. Rose was responsible for five others, counting her mother. She could not get the sad eyes of her children out of her mind, the day she had sat them down, two days before leaving, to explain that what their grandmother had told them about her going away, and may not return, was true.

"Wait a little," Yvonne said, craning her neck to look outside the bus, onto the dark street for her stop, and announced that she was getting off soon.

"You live alone?" Rose asked, concerned for the young woman with the fortitude she lacked.

"No, me live with two other Jamaican women who do live-in work but come home on the weekends. They're here on the domestic scheme program for women from the Caribbean. You know about that?" Gurley said she did, but Rose said she knew little of it and wanted to know more. Yvonne said, "It's not for everybody, you can't be older than thirty-five." Rose wanted to know if one had to work with the employer forever. "No," Yvonne said. "You can work with the family for a year before you look other work elsewhere or stay in domestic work." Yvonne saw that Rose was thinking about it, so she quickly added, "Some women complain of feeling lonely and even isolated, and a lot say they had to work 24 hours round the clock like a slave. And plenty of the employer them racist." Yvonne grimaced. "Me know me couldn't do it." As if Yvonne suddenly remembered this, she said, "The only good thing is that you get landed status when you come through the program."

Yvonne's life intrigued Rose. She couldn't stop thinking that if she had half the determination Yvonne had, she would have sought refuge long before the arguments with her husband led to his physical abuse. Out of concern, and now curiosity, she probed into Yvonne's life.

"Don't worry, Ms. Rose." Yvonne told her that she planned to stay with her brother for the night and for a few days as she had now decided to speed up going to the U.S.

The women exchanged contact information and promised to stay in touch.

Yvonne rang the bus bell, stood, leaned into her two new friends and gave them quick hugs.

Rose thought she saw a smidge of apprehension in Yvonne's goodbye, but a sudden sink in her stomach made her realize that it was her own fear.

Watching Yvonne skip off the bus, the young woman not much older than her eldest daughter Audrey at nineteen, heart-wrenching memories rushed to mind. Audrey was Rose's eldest child, mommy's little helper. During the turbulent marital years when Rose's husband got drunk, he would beat her, and she had to flee to her mother's home for the night, returning the next day when he was sleeping off the alcoholic rage. She had relied on Audrey to take care of the home and her three siblings. Rose saw some of Audrey in Yvonne, that determined spirit, which was comforting, because now Audrey was needed to be the helper for an aging, sickly grandmother, and her curious, energetic, adolescent siblings.

CHAPTER Two

Rose woke up in the middle of the night, shaking from a nightmarish-dream. It wasn't a dream of the lingering thoughts that immigration had her on the run again, but that her children were running wild on the streets of Kingston. Breathing heavily, she wrestled from a feeling of being held under water and sat up in bed. It was a fear she had that once she was gone, they would become wayward, not that they were ever unruly children. Through the fog of half-asleep and half-awake, she fussed with herself. *I didn't raise them that way; they know better*. Although her children becoming vagabonds was farfetched, that did not slow her heart, nor quiet her nerves, she wanted to phone them at 2 a.m. It was not until she convinced herself not to wake them, that it could stay until the morning, did the anxiety pass. Still, she couldn't sleep. She thought of drinking some warm milk but knew that by the time she walked to the fridge and back, sleep would have fully left her eyes. She stayed in bed and not able to quiet her nerves, chastised herself some more with questions: Had she done the right thing in leaving the children with her mother? Even though her mother loved her grandchildren dearly, could her love alone sustain four teenagers when her health couldn't? Her head was clouded with doubt. Unable to relax enough to sleep, she turned on the bedside lamp and took from the drawer on the night table, the one picture she had of them in her passport case; an old black and white photo of a young family in happier, simpler days, the days before they had moved mid-town to their three-bedroom house. Her husband Arthur had had to take on extra shifts as a fireman to maintain the new house when her homebased sewing business could not. Arthur's solution had been to spend more time at the rum bar and then come home and start a fight with her. The old photograph had a tear where in anger she had ripped him out of the picture to rid him from their lives. Now all that was left of him in the photo were his fingers gripping her waist, his body out of sight. Rose often remarked that Arthur had been missing long before she had willed him from their lives. She dropped the photo and felt the stab of regret to her heart; she rolled over, the picture under her chest. Weary, Rose cried herself to sleep.

Rose slept until late morning. She heard rumblings in the kitchen and got out of bed, and not fully rested, surmised that with a nap, if necessary, she could make it through the day. She changed out of her nightclothes and joined Gurley and Cynthia in the kitchen fixing breakfast. "I thought you were going to sleep all day," Cynthia said.

Rose told her that she could not sleep during the night, and ended up falling asleep at the time she should be getting up. "Now my head feels heavy," she said, rubbing the lingering worry from her eyes.

"Well, breakfast is ready, just set the plates and forks for me."

The women sat at the four-seat kitchen table in Cynthia's North York bungalow. The table was pushed to the wall, leaving three seats available for them. Cynthia, strapping, sat sideways so her long legs could stretch in front of her and not under the table playing footsie with the other women. Cynthia and Gurley didn't eat at the dining table anymore and even with the addition of Rose, that never changed. Huddling together in the kitchen made the food more enjoyable, Cynthia often said. As soon as they had finished their liver and bananas, and sat sipping their coffee, Gurley relayed the previous night's events that had her and Rose leaving Pepper Pot Restaurant in a panic.

"You see it," Cynthia said, her face framed by her greying hairline, glasses perched on her nose. She looked and acted older than her fifty-six years. "That's why I don't like going down them places." Her fingers wrapped around her coffee mug. "Too much excitement." She swirled the cup. "That's why I just go in and out." She took a sip of her black coffee.

"But anything can happen anywhere," Gurley said, opening the Toronto Sunday Star.

"Yes, but the possibility is higher there, and you know it."

"I just wanted to show Rose a little bit of Toronto."

"So why you didn't take her to the CN Tower, or to Ontario Place?" Cynthia asked. "Now that would be showing her the sights of Toronto."

"I wanted her to see the city from our end of things."

"From our end..." Cynthia looked askance at Gurley, "From your end it's rough because you put yourself in that position." Cynthia's brows knitted. "And Gurley, you should know better, being so close to getting your papers. You know taking any chance now might mess you up."

Rose and Gurley glanced at each other, and Rose said, "We just stopped to cool off in the restaurant, Cynthia." Her tone pleaded for understanding. "We even had a guy buy us beers," she said, smirking, "Gurley can tell you about that."

"Yes, before the commotion," Gurley said, happy to let Cynthia in on Rose's business. "A man name Roy took a liking", she raised her chin to Rose's direction, "to this one here", and laughed, flipping through the newspaper.

"I know that's why she took you down there," said Cynthia to Rose.

Gurley's head was deep in the newspaper, her focus on the section with the winning lottery numbers. "You hold on there," she said, running her finger down the page, "just let me check my numbers, for all you know I might be sitting on the money to get my house in Rosedale." She burst out laughing.

Cynthia laughed along. "Rosedale? Not even if you won fifty million. People like you and me only go into those neighbourhoods to clean houses."

Disappointed her numbers didn't come up, Gurley sat sulking at another dream lost, although she wasn't deterred by it. Gurley vowed to get two extra lottery tickets for the weekend draw. "After all," she said, "it's them damn immigration officers who spoiled my luck."

Rose cleared the dishes and put them in the sink. She refused to use the dish washer as Cynthia urged. "Me don't believe in machine when me have my two hands", was her reply.

She set another pot of coffee on the table and turned to wash the dishes.

Cynthia topped up her coffee, and as she drank, grew contemplative. She observed Rose from behind; her head down, eyes in the sink, hands in the soapy water, and her mind, nowhere in the kitchen. Cynthia surmised that the reason Rose could not sleep was because she was worrying about her children. She knew Rose well. The two were long-time friends who grew up together as neighbours in the parish of Manchester. Cynthia, ten years Rose's senior, was like a big sister to Rose. She had moved from Manchester to Kingston, Jamaica's capital city, and had encouraged Rose to join her; she had even got her a job at the dress factory she worked. Apart from Mari, Cynthia was the one Rose had confided in during her tumultuous marriage and her plans to take her four children and leave her troublesome husband, after his constant abuse. She was very protective of Rose, often clashing with Arthur over her. Cynthia, so upset when Rose complained that Arthur trailed her from work at nights, and got into a fight with her male co-worker, over jealousy, she knew it was time for Rose to leave the country and leave Arthur all together. She had sent the invitation letter for Rose to visit Canada and hoped that now she could "talk some sense" into Rose to get her to stay.

"Rose," Cynthia called out.

Rose answered "yes", without turning around.

"On a serious note, though," Cynthia continued to say. Rose stopped wiping the counter and turned to face her, holding onto the wet rag. "Regardless of what you experienced last night down at Eglinton," Cynthia said sternly. "I think you should still consider staying."

"At what cost?" Rose said, her wide eyes searching Cynthia's for answers. "I won't tell a lie, Cynthia." She shook her head and sighed. "Last night really bother me."

"Don't let last night deter you." Cynthia took off her glasses, holding it by the handle. "That's one little incident."

"One little incident that almost made my heart come through my mouth," Rose said, trying to hold Cynthia's penetrating gaze.

Rose looked away and fixed her eyes down unto the square tiles beneath her feet. "I can't say right now, I guess we will see how the rest of the trip goes," she said, and turned around and dropped the rag in the sink with a splash and an audible sigh. "Boy, damn if I do and damn if I don't, because it's going to be hard here, same as in Jamaica." Rose's brows knitted in frustration.

"No, Rose," Gurley said, folding the newspaper and setting it beside her on the table. "It's definitely not the same."

"I was running from my husband in Jamaica and come here running from immigration." Rose seemed not far from tears. Cynthia patted the seat beside her for Rose to sit.

"No man, it's only hard until you get settled," Gurley said, trying to convince Rose.

"What do you have to lose?" Cynthia asked, not considering her friend would become an illegal in Canada, and if caught, deported back to Jamaica with no hope of returning.

Rose took a seat at the table with her hand at her jaw. Her dark eyes told her tale.

"It doesn't make any sense you get sad and fret yourself. It's not a hard decision," Cynthia said. She put on her glasses. "The hardest part was getting on the plane, and see, now you're here." Moving closer to Rose, and speaking softly, Cynthia continued. "So, you might as well make the best of what Canada has to offer." With Rose's silence, Cynthia went on. "Jamaica can't help you now, Rose." She shifted from side to side, settling her buttock firmly on the chair. "And things looking to happen with this Trudeau government", referring to Pierre Trudeau's government's hints of an amnesty for illegal residents. "Good things," she said, nodding.

"I know I ain't waiting on no amnesty," Gurley said.

Cynthia leaned forward to stare into Gurley's face. "What do you mean?"

"I mean," Gurley said, tapping the table with her fingers to emphasize her point. "I'll believe it when I see."

"It wouldn't be the first time for an amnesty," Cynthia told her. "It just hasn't happened for a while."

Gurley mumbled again that she didn't believe it had ever happened, and that she had to see it for herself to believe it.

Rose butted in, saying to Cynthia, "So, who said it's going to happen now, anyway?"

Cynthia explained that she had read about the amnesty in one of the Caribbean weekend newspapers a few weeks prior. "It was either Share or Contrast, one of them, me not sure." She regularly picked up the Jamaican-Canadian community newspapers when she shopped at Barry's Caribbean Foods on Eglinton. "As long as you're here for at least two years and never commit a crime, you should qualify," she told Rose.

"Then how does this apply to me who just come here?" Rose asked, desperately hoping there were some facts in what Cynthia was saying.

"Listen, I'm just showing you that things moving in the right direction," Cynthia answered half-heartedly, not wanting to disappoint her friend.

"And, in the meantime I'll have to walk and watch over my shoulder at every turn." Cynthia asked Rose why she said that. "Immigration," Rose responded with a shrug, as if Cynthia shouldn't have to ask. "And I hear that when they catch the people, they deport them with just the clothes on their backs."

"No man, that's a rare occurrence," Cynthia assured.

"It happened, though. I heard stories of people it happened to and they come home with nothing at all, only their two long hands and a bag-a-shame."

"My dear, if you're smart you won't get caught," Cynthia said to Rose, glancing at Gurley.

Gurley rolled her eyes at Cynthia's glance and put her hand at the side of her face, as if to block Cynthia's view.

"Let me tell you something, Rose," Cynthia said, straightening up, "a whole heap of people want babysitter right now, and don't forget some of them willing to sponsor if them like you."

Rose took it all in, pondering all the possibilities to landed status.

"And another thing too, you can always get a man to marry you," Gurley said, her chest jerking from laughter.

Rose gave Gurley "the eye", before she and Cynthia started laughing as well.

CHAPTER Three

The three friends were still in the kitchen bantering and enjoying each other's company, when a knock on the front door interrupted them. They looked at one another, wondering who it was, and why the person didn't use the doorbell. The visitor found the bell and rang it incessantly, causing the women to complain that they were not expecting anyone. At first, Cynthia thought it was the vacuum salesman again, and vowed not to budge because he'd visited the month before and she had told him she wasn't interested. She sat firmer in the seat and continued with her conversation. On second thought, his approach would have been bolder as he knew where to find the doorbell, so bracing one hand on the table, she pushed herself up to go and see.

Gurley, like a mouse caught in a cat's shadow, froze in her seat; the previous night's occurrence was a fresh, unwelcomed memory. Gurley made Rose tense, when she inched to the edge of her seat as if to sprint. She and Rose strained to hear the conversation at the door, and after a minute, they heard Cynthia calling, "Rose, Gurley, come here."

Rose walked ahead of Gurley to the front entrance. What awaited them at the front door caused both women to utter their own versions of surprise. "Girl, what you doing here?" Gurley said, walking toward the woman standing sheepishly next to Cynthia with her back to the closed door, both hands gripping a brown duffle bag in front of her.

Rose moved closer to the young woman. Her face lined with concern for her. She touched her shoulder. "You alright, Yvonne?"

Yvonne had changed from a white blouse and black skirt into blue jeans and a white T-shirt with a red maple leaf on it, the maple leaf visible only in the creases of the T-shirt on her tiny body.

The waitress dropped her bag and turned into Rose's arms. "Ms. Rose," she said, resting her head on Rose's shoulder. Gurley came closer. "Come Miss Gurley." She opened her arms wider, bringing Gurley into the hug. Yvonne was acting as if she knew Rose and Gurley long before their chance experience with immigration one night ago.

The women squeezed into Yvonne's thin embrace, until Gurley first pulled from the hold she had given them. "So, Yvonne," Gurley said, looking her up and down, and at the bag in her hands, "what you really doing here?"

Yvonne pursed her lips in a have-a-little-mercy smile. But it wasn't that Gurley lacked empathy, she had a genuine interest in knowing how she had found them. "You forget we exchanged contact info on the bus last night." Yvonne's voice cracked, suddenly doubting her decision to come to their house. She had forgotten it was her and Rose, and not Gurley who had exchanged contact information.

Rose recognized Yvonne's vulnerableness and put her arm around her. "It's okay, my love. We just thought you were going to your brother."

"I was just passing and said let me stop and say hello." Yvonne eyes moved from one woman to the next, hoping their shared experience at Pepper Pot was enough to accept her showing up uninvited.

Cynthia stood with her arms folded, observing everything, and wondering what this sudden visit from Yvonne meant for her.

"Come have a seat," Gurley said, eyeing her landlady as she passed her going into the living-room. Yvonne stepped out of her rubber flipflops, leaving the slippers at the doorway. Rose carried her bag. Cynthia walked behind them, her arms still folded, her face wearing a frown.

"So, Yvonne, did you go to your brother's last night?" Rose asked, taking a seat beside her on the sofa.

Yvonne clasped her hands in her lap, her feet crossed at the ankles, her bag at her feet. "I was at my brother up 'til this morning." The women surrounded her, waiting to hear why the detour. "But since I left there, I've been walking around wondering where to go, who I could trust, and the next thing I know, I ended up here." A faint smile followed Yvonne's words and she looked down at her hands balled up in her lap.

Cynthia, standing beside the sofa, gazed down at Yvonne, not necessarily buying her story. She said, "You trust them already and you just meet them?", giving Yvonne a side eye. Rose and Gurley glanced at her, seeking compassion for the young woman.

Gurley asked Yvonne, "Did something happen to your brother?"

Yvonne told them her brother wasn't the problem, it was his wife, and that she and his wife didn't get along. The animosity caused her to leave their house. "She doesn't like me," she declared. The women followed up with "why?" Gurley pulled up the love seat; Cynthia leaned against the sofa. Yvonne told them she had got caught up in their domestic problems. Her brother had found out his wife had cheated on him. "The son they have might not be my brother's child." Eight months earlier, when Yvonne had come to Canada she had stayed with them, and one day she had returned home and had found a man in the house with her sister-in-law. Her sense was that her sister-in-law and the man "were up to no good". She had told her brother about what she had seen, and he asked his wife about it, and she denied it. "Ever since, she hates me." Yvonne said she believed her sister-in-law cheated on her brother because he is one of those "softy, soft men", and "it's not the first woman who cheated on him, but he always believed the women". She left her brother's home because his wife was giving her "bad eye" and with the dirty looks, she "didn't want to get poisoned".

Rose and Gurley stared at one another, and Cynthia rolled her eyes at Yvonne's story.

Yvonne's mouth got dried from talking and she continuously licked her lips. Rose brought her a tall glass of water. She watched Yvonne finished the water in one long drink, feeling sadness for her situation, whether the young woman told the truth or not.

Continuing to feel a sense of empathy toward Yvonne, Rose signalled Cynthia and Gurley with a glance. "Ladies, can I have a word in the kitchen?" Yvonne sitting slouched, her eyes on the empty glass in her hands, got up to follow Cynthia and Gurley out the room. "No, not you, Yvonne," Rose said.

Cynthia kept her eyes on Yvonne as she walked out of the room. Yvonne felt Cynthia's gaze and lowered her head. Once the women left the room, Yvonne touched her forehead, her chest and her shoulders in the sign of the cross, then clasped her hand in a silent prayer, *Oh God, please help me*.

The women walked into the kitchen. Rose leaned against the counter, and Cynthia and Gurley faced her with similar baffling expressions. "What is this now?" Cynthia first asked.

Rose remained silent, shaking her head at the telephone receiver.

Roy wasn't deterred by her silence. "From I saw you I knew I wanted to get to know you better."

Rose frowned as she paced in front of the chair, wishing that Roy would just say what he called to say, because she had already deciphered what his intention toward her was from their restaurant encounter. But the cheery pitch in his voice sounded to Rose as if he were drinking, so his call only annoyed her rather than endeared. "So, what you really trying to say?" she asked, impatiently.

"You seem like a nice lady, and I wonder if you wouldn't mind for us...you and me to..."

Rose sighed. *Get to the point or get off the phone.*

"Ahm... to do something one evening," Roy finally got out.

"I can't say right now, I'll have to think about it."

One after the other, the women came to the living room and sat around Rose. Rose rolled her eyes at them, which didn't stop them. Gurley walked by her and whispered, "Remember what I tell you?" and winked. "Be nice."

Rose turned her back to them and less than ten minutes into the conversation, she turned around and asked Cynthia, "You have a pen and piece of paper?"

Cynthia pointed to the small table the telephone was on. Rose took out a pen and calendar note pad, and wrote Roy's phone number on the date they agreed to.

She hung up the phone and shook her head at the women surrounding her, each with a big smile. They wanted to know what Roy said, and Rose teased, "It's none of your business." She explained that he wanted to take her out, maybe to have coffee, or just to talk, and that she told him she needed to confirm it.

"Confirm what? With who?" Cynthia said. "Missus, you're a grown woman, you don't need to confirm with anybody."

"Yes, what you need to confirm?" Gurley asked. "What's stopping you?"

"Missus, go out and enjoy yourself," Cynthia said.

Rose told them that she wasn't asking for permission to go out with Roy, she merely wanted some time to consider it. She dropped to the chair next to her. "Arrrrrhh, it's so quick." Roy hanging onto the bottle of beers, flashed through her mind. "I don't even know him."

"You won't know him until you go out with him," Cynthia said.

"He's a nice guy, Ms. Rose," Yvonne said excitedly. "For the little time I know him, he's always nice to me and encouraged me to keep the faith and that I will see my son soon." Rose stared at Yvonne on the edge of her seat vouching for Roy, and wondered if this person's words were enough for her to feel safe. After all, she had only known Yvonne for a day. "Even this morning, he offered to go and get my things at the restaurant."

"Why not go out with him in a public place, and I don't mean back to Eglinton, little Jamaica," Cynthia said. "Go downtown." She opened her arms and waved to one side. "You can go to Simpsons, they have a nice restaurant down there." She snapped her fingers. "I forgot what floor it's on." She waved her other hand to the next side. "Or Eaton's, they have a nice eating place there too. Go to places where you know immigration not lurking." The women laughed.

Rose chuckled feeling a little excited. "Okay, let me call him back." She called Roy and his phone rang without an answer. She tried fifteen minutes later and still did not reach him. The women encouraged her to try again later. Rose wasn't encouraged, and said, "If he wants to go out with me, he'll call me again."

Rose went to her room and Yvonne followed her there. At the end of the bed was a trunk they sat on. "Ms. Rose, I'm sorry if I was out of place giving Roy your phone number and you don't really know him. But I going to tell you what Roy once told me, 'If you want good, your nose must run.' You have to do the work. Put yourself out there Ms. Rose, everything in life is an investment."

Rose stared at the woman who could be her daughter, giving her advice. "You know my mother told me that same thing when I had to make the decision to leave my children behind."

Yvonne asked Rose about her children and their ages, and she told her they were all teenagers, three girls and one boy. And that they were with her mother, since she and their father were divorced. Yvonne told her, "I know you will miss them, but since you're here now, see this as an opportunity to better help them."

"It would be nice if I could get a job in a dress factory," Rose said, her eyes glistening with hope. She got up and flipped through the few dresses she had hanging in the closet, and took one out, the one she planned on wearing if she heard from Roy. "I made this you know," she said, holding up the dress for Yvonne. Yvonne complimented the embroidery around the neckline. "And the one I had on last night, I made that one too." Rose was awashed with pride, showing off her skills.

Yvonne saw how Rose lit up as she talked about her craft, the brightest she had seen her so far, and understood her pain of unfulfilled desires. She remembered how difficult it was for her to get a job as a stenographer when she first came to Canada even though she had a stenography certificate. Yvonne was willing to do some typing or word processing under the table, if given the chance. Feeling sympathy for Rose, Yvonne offered this as Rose hung the dresses back in the closet, "If you don't get anything in the sewing field, Ms. Rose, try to find something else while you're looking. Because you most likely won't get anything but work under the table, and it's still money in your pocket."

Yvonne's advice hit Rose where she needed it, and she mellowed into the young woman's sound reasoning.

"Ms. Rose, if you want, I can give my boss a call for you."

"Your boss? At Pepper Pot?" Rose scowled at Yvonne's suggestion.

"Yes, since I'm not there anymore, I'm sure he's looking for somebody, because one waitress can't manage."

"But I will be in the same position as you if I go there. And who says that immigration won't raid the restaurant again."

"You can tell Mr. Williams, Bryan, he's the owner, that you have a three-month visa and looking about your landing papers."

"Not sure that will be right, Yvonne."

"Ms. Rose, you have to do what you have to do." Her eyes narrowed when she peered at Rose, giving her something to think about. "Do you think he's paying me the same amount he would pay somebody legal?" Yvonne didn't wait for an answer. "No, so he's looking out for himself too."

"I don't know Yvonne, last night just leave me with a bad feeling about that place." Sitting at the edge of the bed, her heels on the bed rails, Rose leaned forward and rested her elbows on her bent knees. Yvonne sat upright beside her on the bed. "So, I don't feel it would work for me," Rose concluded as she set her feet flat on the floor and faced Yvonne. "But thanks though, young lady." She took Yvonne's hand in hers, the youthful touch reminded her of the tender touches of her daughters, and she remembered the morning they had come to her room to see her getting ready for the airport, and she had wiped the tears from their anxious and worried faces. Marcy, her youngest, had said through her tears, "Mommy we going to miss you very much." In that moment there with Yvonne, Rose wished upon her girls Yvonne's tenacity, courage and wisdom. "You're a good girl, you know that?" Rose said, admiring Yvonne.

Yvonne warmed into a vulnerable child in the presence of the woman that made her miss her own mother, but whose kindness eased the pain of missing her. Rose got quiet and rolled over on the bed, her eyes closed. Yvonne wanted to give her some alone time and said, "I'm going to check out my room. Ms. Rose, if you need me just let me know."

CHAPTER Four

Rose lay across her bed, one bent knee resting on the other, her folded hands across her forehead. All sorts of thoughts floated through her mind, most of all the last time she went out with a man other than her ex-husband. Before Arthur, she had married briefly, just long enough to have Audrey, her first daughter. By the time Audrey had been one year old, the old man she had married had died in his sleep. He had been a farmer, had sold ground provisions to her mother, Mari, at the Coronation Market in Kingston. On his travels there every week, he had seen Rose sitting by Mari's side, and he had started noticing Rose more when her mother had struggled to pay him on time. Mari couldn't afford to send Rose to Madam Beecham Secretarial School as Rose had wanted, so when the old farmer had propositioned, promising to provide for her, it had been an answer to Mari's prayer. Rose had become a wife to the old farmer, filled with hope for his young bride to give him young ones to carry on his "farming dynasty", he often told her. But this wasn't to be, due to pneumonia shortening his life, and their marriage. His death brought Rose relief, not so much for her freedom, but from litigation, as the farm was on captured land. Although Mari had been shame-faced and broken-hearted, offering long apologies when she had welcomed Rose back, Rose held a quiet grudge. Rose had been determined not to let her mother choose her next husband. She had hid her courtship with Arthur until he had proposed. It wasn't until their quarrel and fights, and him throwing her out of the house, and Mari coming to her rescue, taking her and her four children into her one-room tenement apartment that she realized anyone, including her, could make a mistake in judgement. Reflecting on the swindling farmer, and then Arthur, the drunkard, she concluded that she was unlucky with men. The thought soured Rose's countenance.

With her rested hands across her forehead covering her eyes, Rose didn't see Gurley come to the door. "Rose," Gurley called. Rose was startled. She shook off unpleasant memories and sat at the edge of the bed; Gurley sat next to her.

"Why you looking like that?" Gurley said, suspecting what was going through Rose's mind. "I hope you not here feeling sorry for yourself." Rose started blinking to fix a smile in her eyes. "I'm done with the washer and just come to see if you have anything to wash."

Rose took the dress she wore Saturday evening to Pepper Pot, and the pants and blouse she wore to Canada, both hung behind the door, and said, "Only a few pieces", handing the clothes to Gurley.

Gurley looked at the clothes in Rose's hand and back at Rose, sizing up the scenario. "Missus, you think you have a maid here?" she said jokingly at Rose. "Come let me show you how to use the washer."

Rose laughed with Gurley, although a little embarrassed that she was misunderstood. She wasn't taking Gurley for her maid, she had never used a washing machine and thought Gurley was doing her a favour. Smiling awkwardly, she followed Gurley to the basement.

Rose sat in the chair next to the washing machine, her clothes swooshing gently on the delicate cycle. She waited to transfer them to the dryer. Gurley instructed, "They only need 15 minutes on permanent press."

In the meantime, Gurley moved from the laundry room to her room, putting away the clothes she washed and folded. Once she had finished that task, then onto ironing, all a part of her Sunday afternoon preparation for the work week. She set up the ironing board by the window for extra light in the basement, and brought the standing fan from her room and placed it beside her, "for a little cool breeze", she told Rose. Gurley was in her late forties and was already showing signs of peri-menopause, and the ironing was a chore she dreaded but for the breeze from the fan at her back. As she ironed, she engaged Rose about the two jobs she got through an employment agency.

"After I left my son, I was determined I wasn't going back home, Jamaica had nothing to offer me. All I needed was a little job, any work to keep me until I got my papers. Because what I really want is to get a trade, as either a chef or a baker."

Rose agreed that for the short time she had been around Gurley, she saw her passion and talent for cooking and baking. "You would be great at it, Gurley. You could get a little space of your own on Eglinton, or work with someone for starters."

"My dear, don't say that too loud so Cynthia could hear, you know how she feels about being on Eglinton."

"I'm talking about your own business, Gurley."

"Even so," Gurley said. "Anyway, when I got the jobs with the agency," she continued, "I was so happy. Man!" She laughed. "I left my son's house right away as Cynthia had this basement for rent." She told Rose that she never stayed with the employment agency for long. Due to her impeccable work, it didn't take her long to get private jobs. Gurley didn't see Rose raise an eye when she said "impeccable".

For her Monday to Friday job, Gurley provided personal care and companionship to an elderly woman, Irene Mackenzie, who lived at home with her daughter. The elder was confused and for fear of her wandering, she could not be left alone. Gurley arrived at the home 7:30 a.m., just before her daughter left for work. The elder's daughter hadn't considered retirement home or nursing home as an option for her, as her wish was to live at home until death, and she honoured her mother's wish. Gurley was hired to help fulfill this wish. "So, I'll have a job for a long time, definitely until I get my landed." She held the blouse up to check its smoothness, and then placed it on the board again. "Because she is only seventy-seven and it's only her memory that's short," she said, pressing, "she can walk and help herself a little if I watch her." Gurley hung the blouse over the skirt and took it to her closet.

By this time, Rose had put her clothes to dry and went to check on things upstairs. The rudiments of thyme, garlic, onion and pimento seeds titillated her nostrils, leading her to the kitchen. "Something smells gooood," she announced, walking in. Gurley had seasoned the beef from the night before and it was well-spiced and cooking in the oven with a little help from Cynthia.

Cynthia, still sitting at the table, rubbed her elevated knee, and said as Rose entered the kitchen, "Sweeten the carrot juice for me, please?"

Yvonne stood at the counter preparing the potato salad, jumped in the conversation before Rose could speak, "I can do it Ms. Cynthia! I'm almost finished here." She felt helping was the least she could do to show her gratitude.

"Yvonne, you look very at home, you sure you don't want to stay?" Rose said, laughing.

"No, sorry, I'm on a mission, remember?" Yvonne giggled, her youthful confidence on display.

Rose took the grated carrots from the fridge, and all the other ingredients from the cupboard. She held up the condensed milk. "Should I put this in there too?"

"Instead of condensed milk, you know what would give it a nice kick?" Rose stared at Yvonne, waiting to hear the kicking ingredient. "Some whites."

"Rum in the carrot juice?" Rose asked.

"Yes, man, rum nice up any drink."

"No, no, rum would spoil the flavour of a healthy drink like carrot juice." As Yvonne said this, Rose thought of Arthur, this was exactly how he felt about his whites; it was good with any drink, food, even without food. His speciality was white rum straight, which led to nights of drunken ruckus around the house. Rose drew a quick breath and tensed at the memory, and as quickly, shook off the bad feeling creeping up. "I see you're missing the bar too much, Yvonne."

"No way," Yvonne answered, shaking her head. "That you don't have to worry about, Ms. Rose." She smiled, showing all her teeth. "As a matter of fact, I knew this from back home, my father loved it this way. He too loved his rum."

Rose let Yvonne's words flow through her unaffectedly, and feigned a smile, and said, "Let me go get my laundry."

Leaving the kitchen, the spices of back home trailed Rose. Her mother and children preparing their first Sunday dinner without her, brought on a heavy feeling. She stopped on the landing, but before sadness took hold, she reminded herself that her mother went to Coronation Market on Saturday, and the children would have the best Sunday dinner as always, and pushed her feet to keep moving.

Gurley was sitting under the window sewing a button on a blouse when Rose returned. She paused to watch Rose come down the basement stairs, gazing at the ground with each step toward the dryer. "Rose," Gurley called.

Rose's mind far away, she glanced at Gurley and continued to remove her laundered clothes.

"If you want, I can give you the information for the agency where I worked."

Rose nodded slowly, hardly hearing Gurley because of her roaming mind. Gurley didn't wait for her response. "It's downtown, and if I didn't have to be at work for the whole day, I would take you. Maybe Cynthia can."

"What kind of work they do?" Gurley told her housekeeping, including washing and cooking. "For instance, from I go to the house in the mornings, first thing I do is help Mrs. Mackenzie to the bathroom. She's incontinent so I have to get the wet diaper off her." Rose started paying more attention. "Thank God she can walk, because she is a strapping lady and my back couldn't take it." Rose pulled up a chair closer to Gurley, imagining herself in Gurley's job. "After a quick wash, I make her a cup of tea, and while she's having that, I fix her breakfast."

"I could do that."

"Of course you can do it, it's like taking care of your own small children."

Rose sighed and said, "I might not have a choice anyway."

"Darn right. No job should be out of bounds. Forget about the sewing for now."

Rose sighed long. "Boy oh boy, you have to have a strong back for that, because outside of caring for her, keep her from wandering outside, keeping the house clean, you have to do their laundry and cook — everyday?"

Gurley said, "Oh yes." She dabbed her hand along her forehead. Although she sat under the opened window with a little breeze coming in, her face perspired. "Entering the decade of hell," she said and grumbled, "the horrors of menopause."

"So, you have to take care of her and cook too?" Rose said, refocusing Gurley's attention.

"Then how would she eat?" Gurley said and chuckled. "I fix breakfast, lunch and dinner." Rose mockingly asked if Gurley used a microwave to cook, as similar to using a dishwasher, to Rose that was unacceptable. "Microwave? No man," Gurley replied.

"I hear people over this side of the world use the microwave to cook their food, lots of TV dinners," Rose said, jeering.

"No, you watch too much TV." Gurley laughed. "She's a proper Scottish lady. She likes her oatmeal in the mornings, and maybe some potato soup for lunch, and sometimes haggis for supper. I have to feed her, although she doesn't eat that much anymore."

"Hog what she eats?" Rose asked, grinning.

"H-a-g-g-i-s," Gurley said, slowing her pronunciation.

"What is that?"

Gurley told Rose it was sheep's insides. "Then you know how to cook that?" Gurley explained she didn't have to cook it as the woman's daughter cooked it and she warmed it up.

"And you eat Haggis too?" Rose asked, wide-eyed.

"Well, we in Jamaica eat oxtail and cow's feet, don't we?" Gurley snapped back.

"Yes, but that's the tail and feet, not the insides."

"Don't knock it 'til you try it," Gurley said with a wink. "I've tried the haggis once or twice, although I usually bring my own food to work."

"Of course. I know you have to," Rose answered, and both women laughed.

Gurley took up another skirt to iron, and while ironing she said, "Yes, my dear, my days are full from Monday to Friday, until 7 p.m. or so. When I get home, I'm so tired I barely have energy to eat and prepare for bed."

"I'm so used to working from home, it's going to be something to work in people's home."

"You'll get used to it. You'll stay busy as time flies. I don't mind, because private work keeps me out of view of immigration."

"True words," Rose agreed.

"And when I told the daughter that I wasn't straight and looking about my landed papers, she didn't mind."

The arrangement worked out well for the woman's daughter, because she compensated Gurley a small fraction of what the agency used to charge her.

Rose decried, "Cheap labour, that's what I don't like, they treat you like a slave."

"But if you don't have the education or skills for high paying jobs, that's what you have to settle for."

Rose knew Gurley was correct, and she sulked.

"Who knows, maybe if I play my cards right, she'll sponsor me."

Rose nodded and said, "That would be a good break, and the least she could do for you."

"Still, I'm not putting all my eggs into one basket." Rose agreed that wouldn't be wise. "And you know I have the Saturday job with the pilot; that man is very good to me. I even have my own key." Gurley was given a key for her employer's two-bedroom apartment, as he often travelled for days at a time, and was hardly home on Saturdays.

"He's single?" Rose asked playfully, knowing a nice, single man wasn't safe around Gurley.

"Yes, single and handsome you see." Gurley raised her eyes. "A real Rock Hudson look-a-like."

"Maybe you can get him to marry you," Rose said, and a little more serious, added, "you want your papers, right?"

"Yes, but he's not interested in me."

"Why?" Rose looked askance at Gurley. "Many of these white guys love black women, and one that can cook and clean, like you, why not?"

"As his maid, yes, but he's not interested in any women at all." Gurley dabbed her face again. "Not with all them hunky, half-naked men hanging on his bedroom wall."

Rose opened her eyes wide and fell back in her seat, dejected, her sudden hope for Gurley, dashed.

"But he's good to me though, and the work not hard, he keeps his apartment very clean. I just give it the finishing touches, you know, and do mostly dry-clean runs." She chuckled. "And polish and shine his many shoes." She folded the ironing board and leaned it in the corner, leaving the iron next to the board on the floor to cool.

Rose picked up the few clothing she had in her lap and stood to leave. "Well," she said to Gurley, "you have something good going for you, girl, I pray I'll be that lucky."

"I thank God every day, because I hear some sad stories about employers. But God has been good to me so far."

As Rose mounted the stairs, Gurley said she was going to take a little rest.

CHAPTER Five

Later in the evening, after the women had finished supper and cleaned up, Cynthia went to the living room for her weekend ritual: the evening news. On Saturdays it was *W5*, and Sundays, *60 minutes*. She sat in the lounge chair with a cushion at her back, in what used to be her husband's chair. For the last two years of his life, sitting before the television for his favorite shows, he in his lounge chair, and she in the chair next to him holding hands, was one of the little pleasures he could still indulge. Irv Friedman, a widower, was eighty-one years old when he died and seventy-seven the day Cynthia came to him from the agency. They had married in under five months of her moving in as his caregiver. Although Irv's colon cancer had debilitated him with growing weakness and limited mobility, his accountant's brain was ever calculating. Cynthia would give him the Globe and Mail and The Toronto Star after breakfast, and after he had finished reading, he would devour the crosswords. He stayed in his lounge chair day and night, and Cynthia slept in the sofa across from him. She got up in the night to toilet him, and woke up early to feed him so he could take his medication. His two daughters in Montreal and Florida, first objected to their union, but came to accept and appreciate Cynthia for doing what they could not do from afar. In the last few Sundays of Irv's life, he and Cynthia had watched his shows, she had sat by his side and had fed him teaspoons of his favourite ice cream.

Four years after her husband's passing, and the tick, tick, tick, tick, tick of *60 Minutes* loomed, savoury thoughts of ice cream still watered Cynthia's mouth. She got a small bowl of grapenut, and hurried back before the program began.

Yvonne went with Rose back to her room. She had volunteered to put curlers in Rose's hair. Rose sat on the trunk at the end of her bed. Yvonne stood over her to put the rollers in her shoulder-length, processed hair. "Just in case," Yvonne said, "Roy calls and invite you out tonight."

It took a lot of convincing for Yvonne to get this far with Rose. Rose had told her, "'I don't know how much vouching you can do for Roy, 'cause even the thought of going out with a man now makes me queasy."

Yvonne had chuckled. "Ms. Rose, it can't be that bad."

"Ah, my dear, the things you don't know."

"You can't live in your past forever, ma'am, that's history, and history is old story." Yvonne parted a small section of the hair. "You have to step into your future sometime", and stopped to stare in Rose's face, "and Ms. Rose the time is now, time to live some life."

Just then the phone rang.

Gurley came upstairs upon hearing the phone.

Cynthia was still in the living room, slowly eating her ice cream; she got up to answer the phone.

"Listen, listen," Yvonne said, tapping Rose on the shoulder, "I bet it's him calling." She and Rose quieted, listening for Cynthia's call.

Cynthia muted the television. "Rose, Rosie," she called.

Yvonne let go of Rose's hair and said, "Same thing I said." She grinned, proud that she had predicted correctly, and nudged Rose, hoping for a smile.

Getting up, Rose muttered, "Let me see what this man is up to, if he thinks I'm going anywhere with him tonight." She shoved her feet into her house slippers and went out the door. Yvonne trekked behind her.

"Rose, come quick," Cynthia said. The urgency in her voice and eyes scared Rose, and she quickened her steps.

Yvonne and Gurley's smiles straightened, and they drew nearer as Cynthia waved Rose to come. "It's your daughter, Audrey," Cynthia said, pushing the phone in Rose's outstretched hand, and remained beside Rose.

There was a sink in Rose's stomach as she took the phone from Cynthia. She breathed in and exhaled, and recalled that she had spoken with the children and their grandmother the day before and everything was okay, and wondered what could've changed in a day to warrant a call.

"Hello, hello," Rose said, as if on a bad connection, but the only bad connection was the one her mind was sending her heart.

"Mommy?"

"Mommy?" Audrey repeated, her somber voice was almost a whispered. Audrey was making the call from the corner supermarket. In recent years, telephone lines were proposed for the whole neighbourhood, but since the rumour started, there were no movements from the telephone company. After a while, the murmuring residents consoled themselves that it would be sooner than later. They would laugh with each other and comment that everything in Jamaica ran as slow as molasses, so the lines were on the way. Until they get the phone lines, Audrey had to wait in a que with noisy customers surrounding her, just to speak with her mother.

"What is it, Audrey?" The lines between Rose's brows deepened with the racing of her heart.

"Mommy. I just called to tell you that we had to rush granny to doctor this evening."

Rose gasped at her daughter's words. She put her hand on her chest to calm her speeding heart as her eldest daughter relayed that her grandmother had been rushed in a cab to the walk-in clinic a couple blocks away.

"Wasn't Mr. Garrison there to take her?" Rose asked. Audrey told her that their tenant, Mr. Garrison, wasn't at home at the time. Worry overcame Rose. "Who went with her?"

"Me and Maureen, Mommy." Audrey knew where to find the emergency money Rose and her mother stashed away for times like these. "The doctor examined her, gave her medication and sent her home, so she's resting now, Mommy."

"Oh God, oh Lord, Audrey," Rose said, her mind grappling to understand what had transpired since they last spoke. She knew her mother's health wasn't the best, but not that bad to warrant an emergency doctor's visit under three days of her leaving. The decision to leave her four teenaged children with her aged mother took into consideration her worst medical fears, her increased hypertension and arthritis. Her blood pressure was managed with medication and occasional garlic and ginger teas, and she kept her arthritic knee banded and elevated as much as possible. There was no diabetes with a risk of her losing a limb or blindness, so what could have hit her so suddenly? Rose's mouth dried with worry. "So, what you saying Audrey, she just dropped down like that? No warning of a headache and fainting spell?"

"It's like she was worrying, Mommy."

"But what kind a worrying she could be worrying, and I just left there?"

"Since you gone, I catch her in her room, looking out into space, like she's contemplating."

"Contemplating? Contemplating about what?" Guilt brought on anger, then helplessness, and Rose fought back tears.

Audrey didn't have an immediate answer for her grandmother's quiet contemplation, but added that in the morning her grandmother was having shortness of breath and went to lay down. She said her grandmother forced herself to get up and shortly afterwards passed out in the kitchen, and she called a cab to take her to the community clinic. "If you ask me Mommy," Audrey's voice softened, "I believe she missing you, too much."

"But I just left. How—" Rose's eyes zig-zagged, she searched for missing signs, clues that her leaving wasn't well with her mother.

"I believe her heart is broken for you Mommy."

Audrey's words roughened Rose's insides and her insightful comment pushed lingering tears to Rose's eyes. *The children can't manage this.* "Oh God," Rose said, exhausted from the emotional turmoil inside her. Rose was deaf to everything else Audrey said, and her hand dropped to her side, still clutching the phone.

"You alright, Rose?" Cynthia said, standing right up close to Rose.

Rose sighed long to Cynthia's question, nodding, and shaking her head at the same time. Poor Rose was bewildered and overwhelmed. She asked Audrey where her grandmother was, even though Audrey had mentioned that her grandmother was in her room, laying down. Audrey added that her grandmother didn't want Rose notified about what happened to her, but she thought she had to in case her grandmother got worse.

Rose sat in the chair by the telephone to compose herself. "Okay, call me if things change, or I will call first thing in the morning," she told Audrey, a little confused. Audrey agreed. "Everybody else is okay?"

Audrey assured her that they were, only frightened for their grandmother and grateful their worst fears were denied.

Cynthia turned off the television and the women sat around Rose in the living room. Everyone wanted to know what had happened. Rose took a few pensive seconds before saying, "It's mama, she not doing too well."

"Oh Lord, Rose, I hope she alright," Cynthia said; her heart ached for Rose. She knew Mari from they were neighbours back home.

"Luckily the children them big enough to help her," Yvonne said.

"Or they can run and get help," Gurley said.

Rose looked down at the floor and closed her eyes as if silently praying to the Lord. The other women looked on. A short while after, Rose raised her head and said, "I'm not sure if the children can handle the situation by themselves, they never been through anything like this on their own."

"Where is your mama now?" Cynthia asked.

Rose told her that her mother was at home, in bed, and that she had been taken to the doctor, treated and sent home. "Well, okay then." Cynthia tried to console. "The children are there with her if anything, and they will call you if she gets worse and they don't know what to do, or get the neighbour." Rose said that was what she was hoping, that Mr. Garrison wouldn't be too far should something else occur.

"Yes, Ms. Rose, don't worry man, she will be alright, once the doctor sends her home, she's not that bad," Yvonne added.

Gurley forced a smile for Rose and placed her hand over Rose's. "Don't worry, things will work out." Cynthia brought her a glass of water and continued to stand by her side.

Although the women's words calmed Rose somewhat, the situation was still heavy on her mind and she lamented to the women that she didn't know what to do. "Oh, Lord," she said. "Did I make a mistake? Help me."

Rose sat still for a few minutes; the women were quiet too. When she got up, she didn't speak. Locked in her thoughts, she floated to her room.

The next morning, before the stars cleared the sky, Rose awakened. She had slept for eight straight hours after fretting herself to sleep. In the blur between the call about her mother's illness and falling asleep, she hadn't shut the curtains by her bed, and now awake, rolled over to face the dawning of the new day outside her window. She was relieved to not have awakened to another emergency phone call, and thanked God for her mother having another day above ground.

But although she was grateful, bits of the conversation with her daughter, and the worries it brought, crept in. Not wanting to lay there wallowing in a heavy heart, she pushed herself out of bed. Still in her nightie, Rose went to the kitchen. Zombie-like, she entered and instead of turning on the ceiling light, headed to the stove and flicked on the stove-light; she was not ready to be fully awake. She put on the kettle and a pot of water for eggs. Boiled eggs were the quietest to cook so early in the morning without making a lot of clanking and banging of pots to wake up the household. Before sitting to have her coffee, she raised the blinds over the kitchen sink to face the morning's sunrise.

As she sipped her black coffee at the table, looking out the window, memories of a not-too-distant past streamed in. Up until two days prior to leaving Jamaica, and for the last three years, having been forced to leave her sewing machine in her marital home, ending her livelihood as a seamstress, she had taken a job at the Jamaica Omnibus Service (JOS). She had worked the early shifts beginning 5:30 a.m., and her body clock always stirred at 4:15 a.m. It was this early morning rising that had saved her and the children when a burglar had broken into their one-bedroom house as she was getting ready for work. She had heard scratching and shifting at her front door, and curious, she grabbed the flashlight and had drawn nearer. She hadn't yet lit the kerosene lamp she had often used to save on electricity. Quietly, she had inched to the door, and about three feet away, the door had slowly opened, and she had faced a man tiptoeing through the door. Panicked, she had screamed, and had flooded him with a blinding brightness of the flashlight, then turned and ran to the children's bed. The man, also frightened, ran back out the door and through the gate he had left open for a quick escape. Distraught, Rose hadn't gone to work that morning and had still been in shock when the police had arrived. This was one of the incidents that had influenced her decision to try a life abroad.

Rose squeezed her eyes shut to the lightning bolt of memory shooting through her body. She shuddered at the sudden anxiety and chucked down her lukewarm coffee before getting up from the table. Rose just wanted to get to her room should anyone wake up and find her in the kitchen brooding. She quickly rinsed her cup, turned off the stove under the cooked eggs and sped out. Safely in her room, she pushed the door close behind her but it was blocked, a foot had jammed the door.

"Ms. Rose," the voice whispered, "me can come in?" Yvonne was right up on Rose's heels. "Me have something to tell you," she said, hastily. Rose moved further into her room to let her in, giving Yvonne a side-eye that she ignored. "Last night when you'd gone to sleep, Ms. Rose, Roy called you." Rose glared at Yvonne; Roy was the least of her worries. "Him apologized for not calling you earlier, but him said helping his friend took longer than expected."

Rose had forgotten her last conversation with Roy, that he had wanted to take her out after he was finished helping his friend move. Rose knew Yvonne meant well, but the whole idea of her and Roy seemed distant to her immediate concern. "Yvonne, me don't have no time for foolishness right now," Rose said and frowned. "Me have my mother to worry 'bout."

"Me know ma'am, and me sorry to know she not well." Yvonne hung her head, finally heeding Rose's irritation. She slowed her speech. "So, what you going to do?" Rose asked her about what. Yvonne replied, "About your mother."

Rose had not considered which of the many options, going back and forth in her head, she would choose. Nothing she thought of eased her mind, nothing lifted her spirits; every thought reminded her of what chaos might be unfolding at home and why she should be there. Yet the same thoughts reasoned that it benefitted them all if she stayed. If she followed the path of guilt though, she would hop on a plane and return home the next day, but she knew guilt came from fear, and she was not about to let fear of the unknown stop the determined spirit that got her on a plane to Canada in the first place. And as Cynthia had admonished, she was already in Canada, so why not get the best out of it? Rose lowered herself to the edge of the bed. "I don't know Yvonne," she said with a heavy spirit. "My daughter supposed to call and let me know how mama doing."

"Ms. Rose..." Yvonne sat beside her. "I have some cousins in Kingston, I can call them and see if any of them can check on her, for you." Yvonne moved closer to Rose and put her arms around her. "Just let me know, okay," she said. Rose nodded without looking up from the floor, then she fell back on the bed and closed her eyes. Yvonne quietly left the room.

Gurley, on her way to work, came to say goodbye to Rose. She knocked on the door, "Rose, I'm leaving now."

Rose looked at the clock radio on the bedside table; the neon blue light showed 6:25. She cleared her throat and threw her voice through the closed door. "Okay, okay my love."

"Remember what I told you," Gurley said.

Rose squinted, trying to connect Gurley's words from the day before regarding her working with the agency. She called out, "Oh, yes, I remember." After Gurley left, she lay back in bed anticipating a telephone call from her daughter; facing the clock, the time flipped by one minute at a time. Frustrated, she decided "a watched pot never boils", and finally got out of bed and headed to the bathroom. Going into the hallway, she heard an ambulance and police siren sounding increasingly louder as it came toward the home. At the same time Cynthia came from her room, and together they went to the front door. The ambulance and a police cruiser were parked in front of the next-door neighbour's home.

Yvonne joined them. "What happened?" she asked, standing between both women. Rose and Cynthia glanced back at her without answering. "Who live over there?" she pressed.

Cynthia pulled the string tighter around her housecoat, and answered, "An elderly couple", and walked quickly to the fence. Rose and Yvonne stayed at the doorway. Other neighbours came to their doors or peeped through their windows.

A small, silver-haired woman, moving as fast as she could, came from the house to the driveway, her hands flashing and her breath laboured. She waved the two ambulance attendants to follow her, and one of the men pulled a gurney with him.

"Mrs. Pettipiece," Cynthia called. "Mrs. Pettipiece," she said a little louder, trying to get the senior's attention. She parted the shrub to get closer. "Mrs. Pettipiece", but the anxious old lady was focused on the trauma at hand and ushered the paramedics into the house.

Cynthia waited for the few minutes it took the paramedics to wheel Mr. Pettipiece out on the gurney and put him into the ambulance. She looked on helplessly as Mrs. Pettipiece was helped into the ambulance and sat with her husband in the back.

Cynthia did not move from the fence until the ambulance barrelled away and its siren faded. Saddened by the state of her ninety-year old neighbour, she slowly moved from the fence, mindlessly pulling some dry leaves off the shrub with her. The crumpled leaves fell from her fingers with each step.

Inside the house, she gathered with Rose and Yvonne at the kitchen table. Over coffee, she reflected on her neighbour's health. "I feel it, I feel it bad for him. He was so good to me when Irv died. After Irv's funeral when his family left, it was old Mr. P who helped me. Taking me here and there to get things done." Cynthia's chest heaved. "I don't know what I would have done without him and his wife."

"He will be alright Cynthia," Rose said. "Once him get to the hospital, have faith that they will take care of him."

"Yes, Ms. Cynthia, if you say he is a strong, little man, he will bounce back," Yvonne said.

"Well, one thing I can tell you, Mr. Pettipiece is a tough, little cookie. Whatever it is this time, I know he will pull through," Cynthia said, cheering herself up.

Rose couldn't help thinking of her mother after hearing about the sick neighbour. She grew pensive and murmured to herself. "I wonder how mama doing, Audrey supposed to call me this morning." Rose knew the next call from Audrey could determine her fate, if she stayed or went back to Jamaica. Rose sat at the edge of her seat, willing the phone to ring. As if she had channelled her eldest daughter, the phone rang. She didn't wait for Cynthia to get it, she rushed to the living room ahead of her and grabbed the phone. "Hello," she answered, her heart racing.

"May I speak to Rose?"

"Speaking," Rose answered quizzically, taken aback as the voice on the other end was not her daughter.

"Rose, this is Suzy Fong, from Fong's Supermarket." Suzy was the owner of the grocery shop at the top of Summerfield Road where Rose's family lived; it was one of the few establishments that had a phone for hire.

Rose began pacing; *why is Suzy calling me?* Her eyes zoomed in and out, bringing into focus Suzy's round, olive-toned face, her slanted, brown eyes and long, straight, black hair, newly greying. A white t-shirt with black pants, Rose would bet that was what Suzy was wearing. Rose put her hand to her chest, her heart pulsating under her palm. "Oh, Ms. Fong, how…how comes you're calling me?"

"I'm calling for your daughter Audrey, she asked me to give you a message."

Rose stopped moving. She leaned her head into the phone. "Yes, go ahead."

"You know we don't open the shop until 9 o'clock, but—" Rose glanced at the clock on the wall, above her head, it showed eight-thirty. The Chinese business owner lived in a Kingston upper-class neighbourhood. The business woman owned, along with her family, the grocery shop, with an adjacent auto body shop, located in the lower-middle class neighbourhood. The establishments were passed down by their parents. Suzy came to the shop every morning around 8 o'clock and stayed upstairs until it was time to open the supermarket. Rose imagined Audrey knocking on the side entrance of the building to get Suzy or one of the family members' attention and hoped that their two Rottweilers weren't ruffled too much by Audrey's knocking.

Suzy continued, "Because Audrey had to rush off to school before we opened, she asked me to call and let you know that her grandmother was feeling better."

Only somewhat relieved, Rose asked, "So, you know if mama is there by herself?"

"Audrey said the people from across the street, can't remember their names now, would give an eye."

"Must be the Roberts," Rose answered. Although she did not inform anyone in the neighbourhood that she was leaving the country, the Roberts family were the closest to her family and would give an eye.

"Yes, yes," Suzy said. "The Roberts, their helper Veronica will check in on her."

Mari and Mr. Roberts' mother were close. The two older women went to the same church and often travelled together. Rose suspected that her mother may have told her old confidant the details of Rose's absence.

"Okay, okay then," Rose said to Suzy, a little more upbeat.

Suzy said, "Don't worry man and Audrey said she's not staying long at school today, she only has two morning classes."

Rose thanked Suzy for delivering the message. "Before you go, tell me something. You have any idea when the phone company going to install phones in the area?"

"Yes, I hear it should happen in a couple months."

"Well, we know in Jamaica a couple months can mean up to six." Rose and Ms. Fong laughed.

"No man," Ms. Fong said through laughter. "No seriously, I see the JTC truck coming around and the guys checking out the poles."

Rose was thrilled and answered, "Well if that's the case, that's great, because it's needed badly down there." Suzy agreed with Rose, which only encouraged her. "These are modern times, so Jamaica must catch up with the times. Why shouldn't everybody have a phone in their home?" The force with which these words left Rose's mouth surprised her, and in that instant, going back to Jamaica to live, lost a little more certainty.

Suzy began to say something, then hesitated. Rose had a feeling what it was and quickly said, "Okay, I hope Audrey call me soon. Thanks Ms. Fong, bye, bye."

Suzy, emboldened by the call ending and her chances slipping away, said, "So you coming back?"

By Rose's non-response, she knew she had waded into forbidden territory. How could Suzy not have been sensitive to a question such as that, especially over the phone?

"Anyway, that's not my business," Suzy replied, shoveling herself from out of her indiscretion.

Rose answered, "Please tell Audrey to call me, thank you."

Chapter Six

For the rest of the day, Cynthia looked out for her neighbours, wondering how Mr. Pettipiece was doing. She did her chores and returned to the chair by the window, watching for movements in and around their bungalow. She had grown fond of the old couple from the first day her husband Irv had introduced them. He had been in the backyard uprooting the last batches of vegetables, before the first frost; one of the few pleasures he could still do. The old couple had been in their backyard and Irv had chatted with them across the fence.

Cynthia, his new caregiver, came to see that her elderly employer was not overexerting himself, and he introduced his neighbours to her. When they discovered that Cynthia was from Jamaica, Mr. Pettipiece said, "The land of sun and rum", licking his lips and laughing haughtily. Mr. Pettipiece told Cynthia that he and his wife had been to Jamaica many times in their younger years in Bristol, United Kingdom. His brother, an engineer, went to Jamaica on a work project and ended up living in the parish of Portland. From that day they met, and

Mr. Pettipiece saw Cynthia, he would relay a different, or the same, story of places he had been in Jamaica, places Cynthia had never been to, like the top of Blue Mountain with temperatures that reminded him of autumns in England. It pleased her to see the twinkle in his blue eyes reminiscing about her homeland, and a little jealous of his experiences that she was too busy carving a better life to explore. By the following year, Irv married Cynthia at City Hall and invited Mr. and Mrs. Pettipiece over for tea, and his favourite Jewish treat, chocolate rugelach made by his new wife with a little added rum, specifically for Mr. Pettipiece. Mr. Pettipiece told Cynthia then that he was genuinely happy that she no longer had to worry about her landed status and returning to the land she loved, but which could not offer her the lifestyle to which she had become accustomed. Little did he know that her not going home would one day mean much more to him.

Tears came to Cynthia's eyes remembering her neighbour, and she inched closer to the window as a car pulled up in their driveway. The driver got out of the car and went around to the other side to help Mrs. Pettipiece from the car. Wrapping his arm around hers, he led her inside the home, and returned to the car shortly after, and drove off.

Cynthia quickly went to the kitchen and dished some beef soup in an aluminum canister. Gurley was not home, Yvonne had gone on the road, and only she and Rose were home. "I'm going to check on Mrs. P," she said sticking her head in Rose's room. "You want to come?"

Cynthia and Rose walked up to the neighbour's porch and Cynthia rang the doorbell. It occurred to her waiting at the door that the last time she entered the Pettipieces' home was the time she had visited sick Mr. Pettipiece. Her heart sank remembering, and sadness welled up in her.

Mrs. Pettipiece came to the door in a yellow sweat suit Cynthia had seen her wear on many occasions, the bright yellow had faded to pastel. She once told Cynthia it was her favorite outfit. Unlike her sweat suit, her pearl white hair was newly done. Mrs. Pettipiece was known for freshly done, in-place curls. Only this day, the tightness of her curls could not lift the solemnness from her face. Mrs. Pettipiece stood in the doorway, holding unto the doorknob. "Come in, my dear." Sorrow weighed on her still recognizable British accent.

The women entered the home. Rose quickly observed her surroundings. On the centre table was a lit cigarette in the ashtray, the smoke rising in slow circles, filled the air. Rose coughed. Cynthia glanced at her and said, "This is my friend Rose visiting from Jamaica", and motioned to the bag in Rose's hand.

Rose gave Mrs. Pettipiece the soup and she received it with trembling hands and a strained smile.

Rose wiggled her nose and frowned at the irritating fumes. She covered her mouth to stifle a surge of coughs.

Cynthia scolded her with a quick side eye, *control your coughing* and turned back to Mrs. Pettipiece. "I brought a little soup for you ma'am," she said. Cynthia took the soup from Mrs. Pettipiece and carried it to the kitchen.

Mrs. Pettipiece offered Rose a seat on the couch, close to the smoke-filled ashtray. Rose coughed and fanned the smoke from her face. Mrs. Pettipiece smiled apologetically, and reached over the table to put out the cigarette.

Cynthia returned from the kitchen and saw the two women sitting silently next to each other: Rose as if holding her breath and at any moment would burst, and Mrs. Pettipiece with her knees together, hand in her lap, as if afraid to move, fiddling with the married ring on her finger. Cynthia thought that Mrs. Pettipiece appeared much frailer than usual. Cynthia sat on the other side of Mrs. Pettipiece. "I'm not staying long, Mrs. P," she said. "I just wanted to hear how Mr. P. doing."

"Not well. They admitted him at the hospital."

"Oh God, sorry to hear," Cynthia said, slumping into feelings of pity for poor Mr. Pettipiece. "What did they say was wrong?"

"Same thing, same goddam thing," Mrs. Pettipiece said, shaking her head in disgust.

"The smoking?"

"Yes," Mrs. Pettipiece answered sharply, her face hardening. "I don't know what's going to make him quit." Cynthia glanced at the cigarette butts in the ashtray.

"Maybe this time he will," she assured Mrs. Pettipiece. "He stopped the drinking cold turkey when his doctor advised him to, so maybe he'll stop the smoking now for good."

Mrs. Pettipiece frowned and shaking her head, said, "I really don't know." She thought of the many times she had begged him. A heavy smoker, her husband had been rushed to the hospital earlier in the year due to shortness of breath. He had been diagnosed with chronic obstructive pulmonary disesase and kept in the hospital for over a week. He hadn't been sent home until he was weaned off oxygen and warned to give up his smoking habit. The scare caused Mrs. Pettipiece, also a smoker, to quit. She had started up again when her husband had picked up his old habit, shortly after he had returned home from the hospital. His family doctor had put him on home oxygen, which still hadn't prevented him from smoking.

"And this isn't good for me," Mrs. Pettipiece said, worry enlarging the vein on her forehead. "Because, every time he goes to the hospital and comes home, he comes back worse, and it's getting harder for me to manage him."

"Do you know when he's coming home, ma'am?"

"Who knows at this point," Mrs. Pettipiece answered, and started pacing about.

"Are you okay, Mrs. P?" Cynthia asked.

Mrs. Pettipiece sighed and replied, "I'd better go and take a shower. My godson's coming to take me back to the hospital shortly. I'm staying overnight."

"Maybe you could have a little soup before you go."

"I'll try," she said, her voice quivering. "I've lost the little appetite I had."

"You have to eat ma'am to keep up your strength for both you and him."

Mrs. Pettipiece nodded in agreement, but still looked worried.

Cynthia and Rose got up to leave and Cynthia walked over to Mrs. Pettipiece and hugged her. "Can I do anything for you before I leave, Mrs. P.?" The senior told her thanks, but no. She explained that she had to get ready to leave again as her godson was coming soon. "Okay, but let me know if there's anything you need." Cynthia gently rubbed her neighbour's shoulder. "If there is anything I can do, just call me. You still have my number?"

Mrs. Pettitpiece shuffled on the spot, bringing to memory where she might have placed Cynthia's number. Remembering, she raised an eye, and went to the kitchen. She opened a drawer filled with papers and ruffled through it, until she found the paper with Cynthia's number that she had given her the last time Mr. Pettipiece was in the hospital. She brought it out, waving it at Cynthia. "Here it is."

"Good, please use it, Mrs. P.," Cynthia said, and walked with her to the door, Rose behind them. "Tell Mr. P. I'm praying for him. Please call me and let me know when he's coming out, so I can pay him a visit before he does."

In the driveway, out of the earshot of Mrs. Pettipiece, Cynthia said to Rose, "Poor soul, I feel so sorry for her, for you know he's going to be a handful."

"It's only the two of them? They don't have any children?"

"They have a daughter in the U.S. and a son who lives in

Australia with his family." Rose looked a Cynthia questioningly and said, "But they're at the stage in life where they're going to need their children."

"Children over this side of the world are more independent, they're not afraid to move away from their parents, and the telephone or a post card every now and again is their line of communication."

"She mentioned a godson," Rose said.

"Yes, one of her dear friend's grandson. But he's in university, he's not going to have the time to help them every day."

"It's hard because them old and alone," Rose said, her mind creeping to her own mother at home.

"I know," Cynthia said. "She won't be able to manage her husband coming home in a worse condition, and she can hardly manage herself as it is." Reaching her gate, Cynthia stopped and said, "This will be the perfect job opportunity for you when Mr. P. comes out of the hospital." She did not see that Rose had slowed her walking and was looking away. Rose was focused on the heavy smoking that would entrap her in their house.

Cynthia waited for Rose to catch up. She made sure to look into her eyes, and said, "Right Rose?" If she detected Rose's disinterest, she pretended not to, and continued, "This is exactly what you need, two old people to look after. That's stable work. Even if Mr. P. pass away soon, you'll still have Mrs. P., who is looking quite frail." Rose's silence did not deter her, and Cynthia said, "That shouldn't be too hard." Cynthia meant well, even if she was ignoring Rose's asthma.

"I guess so," Rose replied, nonchalantly.

CHAPTER Seven

The night before Yvonne planned to go to America, this happened: Cynthia, Rose and Gurley waited for her to join them, no doubt, Yvonne thought, for a last attempt at convincing her to ditch the plan for illegal entry into the U.S. "Tomorrow I'll be with my honey bun, and I can't wait," Yvonne said, waltzing into the living room, grinning as if already in Brooklyn. She dropped to the carpeted floor, buttocks first with her legs crossed. Her fingers clasped, she prepared for their interrogation.

"So, you're ready for your new life in New York?" Rose said from the couch.

"Of course!" Yvonne replied with a wide smile and eyes of liquid joy. She hugged her bent knees to her chest and rocked back and forth.

"You mean to ask," Gurley sitting next to Rose on the couch chimed in, "Is she ready for her big escape across the border?"

"Ready as I'll ever be," Yvonne said to Rose, ignoring Gurley's sarcasm. "I made up my mind long ago, and it's do or die." A seriousness came over her and she sat up with a calm resolve. "I'm going."

Gurley looked askance at Yvonne. "You know there are other ways, legal ways," she admonished.

"I don't have the money or time for that."

"Missus, all I can say is, you're very brave," Gurley said.

Rose stared at the young maverick, searching for signs of apprehension, and detecting none, smiled in awe.

Cynthia sat quietly until now; she leaned forward in the lounge chair. "That's a hell of a task you planning to undergo young lady, travelling how many hours by yourself in the jungles of New York." She peered over her glasses, penetrating Yvonne's determination. "Are you sure you can handle the streets of New York City?"

"If anyone can, it's Yvonne," Rose said, trying to take some of the heat off the young woman she had grown protective of like a daughter.

Yvonne hardly needed help. She quipped, giving as much as she had been getting, "Absolutely! I know I can. There's lots of opportunities there and I'm ready for any one of them." She braced backward on her hands. "Remember though, I'm not going to be alone. My boyfriend has a whole heap of family over there, not only in Brooklyn, even Bronx." She caught a breath and lowered her voice to a strong conviction. "I only want to get there, and I'll be fine."

"I didn't say there weren't good things about the place, but it's the crime, man." Cynthia rolled her eyes. "And there's not a day that goes by that an illegal person don't end up in trouble and deported home. Just the other day," she continued, determined to state her case for the risk Yvonne was undertaking, "Mr. Louis' two sons went up to their mother in Bronx, and before you know it, they join gangs and got caught selling drugs and sent to jail, and when them serve them time, they were deported back home to Jamaica." Cynthia scowled in disgust, and satisfied that she had pleaded a strong case, sat back, and glanced at Rose and Gurley for agreement.

"That won't be my experience, Ms. Cynthia, because I won't be with anybody who shooting up or selling drugs." Yvonne's tone was heavy from her defending herself and it bordered on anger. "What about the people who go there and make better for themselves? One of my boyfriend's nephews, got a scholarship for New York University."

Yvonne's counter left the women quiet.

"Well, my child, I can't tell you what to do," Cynthia said, bracing the arms of her chair to get up. "And I know you want good for yourself, so I just wish you all success. You are a smart, young woman and if I was a betting woman, I'd put money on you." Cynthia stood. "Anyway, I'm going to bed." Walking away, she turned, and asked, "What time are you leaving?"

"The driver coming to pick me up at 5:30."

"Daylight?" Rose quickly enquired.

"Yes, he said nighttime would seem more like we sneaking across."

"Alright." Cynthia's chest heaved quietly, she had done as much as she could, she had to let Yvonne live her life. "I might be sleeping at that time, so, God go with you." Cynthia disappeared into the dimmed hallway.

Gurley got up next. "What can I say, my dear?" She looked at Yvonne with curious adoration. "You made up your mind, so good luck and God bless." She walked away. "I have the people them work to attend to in the morning, so —" her voice trailed off.

Relieved that Gurley and Cynthia had left the room, Yvonne shuddered with a sigh of relief. She lowered her head between her bent knees and stayed that way until Rose, sitting behind her on the couch, said quietly over her shoulder, "It'll work out man, have faith."

Yvonne raised her head and for the first time Rose didn't see that jubilant glow engulfing her. "You're okay?" Rose asked.

"Just tired, tired of constantly defending myself."

"Well, the decision is yours and God's alone, so at the end of the day you'll have to please yourself." Yvonne nodded. "Only you and the driver going?"

Yvonne said she wasn't sure. "All I know is that he is coming to get me in the morning and we're heading straight to the border." Yvonne shook her head. "I don't even know which border."

Rose tapped the empty space on the sofa and Yvonne pushed herself off the floor and sat beside her. As Yvonne stared at the floor, the pulse in the side of her head pounded.

Rose cupped Yvonne's hand with hers and gently said, "You nervous? You can tell me, you know."

Yvonne shrugged and said, "Why get nervous now? It's too late for that." She parsed her words, saying, "I just have to not let the negative vibes get to me."

"I'll tell you what my mother always told me, why worry when you can pray?" Yvonne raised the corner of her mouth in a half smile. "My dear, this is the time when you have to trust God, for only him and him alone can guide you."

Yvonne appreciated Rose's words and nodded slowly as it soaked in. She felt lighter and turned to Rose. "By the way, how things with your mother? You heard from home?"

"Yes," Rose answered. "I finally talked to Audrey yesterday when she came from school." Audrey had worked it out with the neighbour that their helper would give an eye on her grandmother when she and her siblings were gone to school, until her grandmother was better to go back to work.

"I really want things to work out for you too, Ms. Rose." Yvonne felt close to Rose and she held Rose's hands in hers. "Once I get set up, if things don't work out over here, you can always come to the States, and I will help you." Rose smiled, she considered Yvonne such an inspiration. "I have the job set up to go into, as I told you, so I can see if they need anybody."

"The garment factory?"

"Yeah, and like how you can sew, they make all kinds of uniforms, you could probably get a job there."

"That would be ideal to tell the truth," Rose said, and lowered her head.

Yvonne lifted Rose's head by the chin. "What is it Ms. Rose? Something wrong?"

"Cynthia trying to set me up with the sick people them next door, Mrs. P. and her husband, but me can't take the whole heap of smoke. Yesterday I was over there and almost get an asthma attack. Me almost pass out stopping my breath," Rose said.

Yvonne chuckled.

"Ms. Cynthia can be forceful, if she wants you to do something, she can be very persistent."

"You see it too, right?"

"Oh yeah, me notice that long time. Look how she was with me tonight."

"I don't want to go home," Rose said. "I want to stay here and help my children and my mother, but at what cost? The smoke would kill me over there."

"Well, you don't have to rush into any answer now. You have other options. Another thing to," Yvonne stood. "Roy wants you to give him a call. Him asked me to even phone him and put you on the phone. Him don't want to lose the connection with you when I'm gone." Rose hissed. "Him really like you, Ms. Rose, and don't forget him single and straight, so that could be an option right there."

"Come go to your bed, don't forget you have an early morning and a long day ahead of you," Rose told Yvonne, ignoring what she had said about Roy.

Even though it was Yvonne who was travelling, Rose couldn't sleep, and when Yvonne came to her room carrying her duffle bag at approximately 5:20 a.m., she was awake. Rose's door was slightly ajar, and Yvonne put her head in. "Ms. Rose, Ms. Rose," she said. Rose sat up in bed. "It's time now Ms. Rose, the man come." Yvonne's voice cracked, it was a bittersweet moment for her.

Rose met Yvonne at the door and her eyes were watered to see the young woman ready to leave for an unknown journey. She hugged Yvonne. "Travel safe, my love. God go with you."

"Tell Ms. Cynthia and Ms. Gurley goodbye for me."

"You want me to see if they are awake?"

"No, don't bother to call them, they're probably still sleeping."

"Alright," Rose said, walking Yvonne to the front door. They hugged again and wished each other all the best. "Call me, alright."

"I will link you once I reach and everything is copasetic," Yvonne said and winked at Rose. Rose squeezed Yvonne's hand and watched her hurry to the waiting dark grey Honda sedan. One last wave from the back seat of the car and Yvonne was gone.

CHAPTER Eight

The afternoon Yvonne left for New York, the women sat in the living room reminiscing over her stay with them. Although they each had their own experience and takeaway about her, the one thing they all agreed on was her tenacity, her bravado to do just what she set out to do. They wished her all the best for the future and Rose led them in a short prayer for her. "Well," Rose lamented, "Yvonne said she would call when she reached her destination to let us know if she reached safely, so I hope that's not too long." She sighed. "I can't wait to hear from her that everything is okay."

A heavy thumping sounded on the door and the women looked at each other, *who is this now*? Cynthia wondered out loud if it could be Yvonne returning after an unsuccessful attempt at the border. She got up to go see if it was the young woman at the door when Gurley stopped her. "Cynthia, that sounds like a man's knock, look through the peephole first." Gurley positioned herself to run to the kitchen. She had a habit of always being on edge, even in the house, due to a possible impromptu visit from immigration.

At first Rose also thought it was Yvonne returning. Fears of an unsuccessful trip of interrogation, shame and possibly deportation for Yvonne shook her. Gurley's anxiousness didn't help either, and Rose panicked. Yet, it didn't make sense to be nervous because she was still two weeks under her three-week stay in the country. But stories of immigration officers showing up at no appointed time to residences, searching for illegals, and shipping them home, distorted her thinking. Crazy, mixed-up thoughts took hold: going home as a deportee would be shameful, and even worse, going home with no money, and no option of returning would be sad. She sat at the edge of her seat, listening quietly, breathing lightly. The voice at the front door was a man's, with an accent, a Jamaican twang, which should've relaxed her, but it didn't. Immigration using Jamaicans as spies, to her in that moment, wasn't far-fetched. Even so, she wasn't relaxed enough to laugh at her foolish thinking; fear made her imagination seem real.

It was a long two minutes. The front door closed. The person had entered the house. Cynthia returned to the dining room carrying two plastic bags. "It's Norman," she said, smiling. "My friend from home."

Rose's chest heaved slowly and she relaxed. When Cynthia continued to the kitchen, she leapt to her feet to follow; Gurley was already in the kitchen hiding.

Gurley came from behind the door, and embarrassed, she shrunk into a toothless smile. "You can't be too careful," she said.

Rose chuckled, hiding her own fright. Cynthia grinned, she was used to Gurley's dodging and hiding.

Cynthia handled the bag with the three bottles of liquor: a Wincarnis, a Stone's Ginger Wine and an Appleton Rum. She gave Rose the other bag with Julie and East Indian mangoes. Rose washed them and put them in the fruit basket on the counter. The mango aroma took Rose back to the days she sat with a bowl full of them in her lap, listening to her mother's pigeons in the back yard.

Cynthia, with Gurley and Rose in tow, went to the living room where Norman waited. Cynthia carried the two wines, Rose the rum, and Gurley a tray with the glasses that were laid on the centre table. Cynthia sat beside Norman on the couch with his hat hanging off his bent knee. She introduced the women, also sitting, Gurley at the other end of the sofa and Rose in the loveseat. "You remember Gurley, right?" Norman said he did, and Gurley said she remembered him as well. "And that's my friend Rose," she said to Norman with her gaze on Rose. "She came up nearly a week ago, and already she wants to go back home. You ever heard anything so stupid?" Cynthia frowned and continued, "Before she stay here and earn some money to send home."

"Well, maybe she has a husband going back to," he answered, his elbow on the arm of the sofa, his face resting on his fisted hand as he eyed Rose. Norman's mention of Rose having a husband was to determine if she had a husband, for he was quietly admiring Cynthia's younger friend.

"Which husband?" Cynthia snapped. "She left that bastard long time." Everyone laughed, except Rose.

Cynthia's words riled Rose and she flatly responded, "I did have a husband, yes, I did." Her tone strong and affirming, "And he was a good man, when he wasn't drunk."

Cynthia interrupted, "Anybody ready for something to drink?" Her abrupt interruption was deliberate; however, her question went unanswered as the others were too engrossed in what Rose had to say.

Rose glared at Cynthia for cutting in as she spoke. She knew that Cynthia didn't like Arthur, but still thought she had acted rudely. "As I was saying," Rose smirked and continued, "my husband was a fireman." Her voice raised with pride remembering how impressed people were of his profession. "And a good provider, me and the children never went hungry." Her eyes dimmed a bit. "It's just that he had a problem," she said, mostly convincing herself. "He had a sickness, that's why him drink all the time." Although the others remained quiet, she saw doubt on their faces. She put her hand to her jaw. "I believe…" her words were muffled. She removed her hand and shifted in the seat. "I believe it was moving from the tenement and suddenly having the responsibility of a new house with four small children to care for, that put so much pressure on him."

"Rose!" Cynthia yelled across the room, "stop making excuses for that man, you know him was no good. For no good man beat him wife like how him beat you."

Without looking at Cynthia, Rose kept talking. "He would keep things inside, and when him drink too much white rum, him was like the devil himself, and take out him frustration on me." A faint smile crossed her face. "They say you only hurt the ones you love." Cynthia burst out laughing. Rose ignored her. "It was like a demon let loose in him that he could only control by fighting with me." Her chest heaved and sank, her voice was shaky. "I couldn't take the bad living anymore because the fighting would terrify the children, and I couldn't stand to see them crying all the time, I had to take them and leave." She bit her lip to stifle her tears.

Everyone's face grew long. Cynthia got up, announced that it was time to lighten the mood, poured a glass of Wincarnis for Rose and put it in her hand. Norman said he wanted Wincarnis, same as the women. Cynthia joshed that he was getting soft. He then appeased her and requested rum with orange juice. "That's more like it, brother Norm," she said, then raised her glass. "Here's to making decisions." They all lifted their glasses to Rose.

"I believe the grass not always greener in the neighbour's yard. Sometimes it's just envy and greed colour it so," Norman said, to nods of agreement. And speaking to Rose, he said, "Jamaica can work. It can work if you know how to make it work for you. I mean, with my farming, I was able to open a dry goods store, and I have a man who go to town with some produce on weekends, and that's all doing just as well."

As Norman spoke, his words encouraged Rose, and a thought brightened her eyes. She smiled wide-eyed and said, "I totally agree. I was a dressmaker for many years, and if I went back, I could probably make it work again." Her head bobbing, she seriously contemplated the possibility.

"Missus, stop your nonsense," Cynthia said, waving her down. Rose jerked backward, shocked at the flash of Cynthia's hand. "You know the dressmaking business hard nowadays. People want designer clothes even if it's imitation, as long as it's a so-called brand name they can buy in a store." Rose's eyes burned. Restraining herself, she listened as her dream ended as soon as imagined. "And you know business was bad. That's why you had to take the job at the bus company." Cynthia's eyes locked on Rose's. "Be real now, Rose!"

Rose winced at Cynthia's stabbing words: all she'd done was dream out loud. The wine heated her blood, not a usual drinker for this reason, it loosened her tongue. She set the glass on the floor beside her and sat forward in the chair, gripping the arms. She said, "Cynthia, no, you be real! Try to see things from my end for a change." Cynthia pulled back, her eyes widened and her mouth hung open. "Not because you don't have a chick nor a child to concern you, and fortunate enough to have a man leave you a house that's paid for, and money to do whatever you want." Her chest rose and sank in a quiet rage. "Well, it's not so for me. I have four children and a mother depending on me. I can't fail them!" Rose said firmly. "I have to make sure that every move I make is the right one."

The words came out stronger than she intended, but she couldn't stop now. "Everything in life is not a snap decision. People's lives at stake here." She swayed in her seat. "My mother is not a healthy woman. It's a chance I take leaving her with this extra responsibility."

Cynthia shut her mouth and sat back in her seat. She knew that as much as she could give, her younger friend, when pushed, could push as hard, and she had pushed her beyond her boiling point. She folded her arms, pursed her lips and allowed Rose to vent. "Maybe if you had people depending on you, you'd think differently. Give me a chance, man! Let me think things through. This is a big gamble for me, you know." Rose pointed at herself, and said louder, "And it's me, me alone, who have to make this decision!" The swirling ceiling fan, was the only brave sound to follow Rose's rant.

Cynthia got up, holding her glass, she faced everyone. "Listen," she said, in the uncomfortable space. "Not everybody would do what I did to stay in this country." Now all eyes were on her. Gurley and Norman, who knew most of Cynthia's story, didn't lean in like Rose. "Yes, I met a man with money, and yes, he was twice my age, he took a liking to me and helped me go back to school for my nurse's aide certificate. But I still worked. I wasn't going to live off him." She shrugged. "I wanted my own, and as nice as his two daughters were to me when I was taking care of him, after he died it was a different story." She placed the empty glass on the centre table and said, "Because don't forget, you know, from his wife died, it's like he was dead too, until I started taking care of him and brought him back to life, and with all this, they gave me hell." She shook her head and sighed heavily. "They even took me to court to take this house from me." She sat on the arm of the sofa, scooting Norman over. "But thank God, Irv Friedman never left me out of his will, God rest his soul." She pointed to the floor at her feet and said, "None of them two girls, none of them, could take what was rightfully mine!"

"No one could begrudge you of that Cynthia," Rose said, her voice hoarse and low. "For that is your fortune here in this country. That doesn't mean that my journey should or will be the same. Because, as you said, not everybody going to do what you did. Some of us would rather go home than make people take liberty with us," she said painfully. "And you can't even walk freely, you have to constantly look behind you for immigration." The others looked on sympathetically as Rose spoke.

Norman shifted himself on the couch and leaned forward; Cynthia got more room next to him. Norman said, "I know how you're feeling, Rose. I was once in a predicament like you, about twenty years ago, I had to make a decision to defy my father." His voice got stronger. "I didn't come here by choice. I didn't run away from Jamaica either. It was my father. He sent me to live with one of his brothers who was living in England and then moved here," he said and coughed. "He got a white woman pregnant, and they got married. My father wanted me to have the opportunity he never had, so he shipped me away after high school to my uncle here in Canada." He coughed again and Cynthia offered him some water, he requested the water without ice. He drank some and continued. "Me, I couldn't stay here, man. It was too darn cold," he said and laughed, and they all mumbled their agreement of living in an "icebox". "Plus, I had a girlfriend who had just finished teacher's college. We had planned a life together and I missed her, real bad. So, no matter what my father said, or my uncle, I knew I was going back home." Rose asked how long he stayed in Canada. He drank the rest of the water and didn't go back to the alcohol. "I stayed here a few years to earn some money to take back home; I was looking at marriage for me and my girlfriend. So, my uncle got me a job at the factory where he worked. The pay was good, but that still couldn't change my mind to stay. The men at the job were really prejudice, called me damn nigga and all them things, which didn't deter my plans."

The telephone rang and Norman paused, his eyes trailed Cynthia across the room. It was his nephew calling to say he was coming to pick him up at 9:30 p.m., in half hour. "Tell him that's okay, man," Norman said. From Norman's uncle died, he stayed with his son and his family when he came to Toronto to buy new equipment or products for his business. "One time," he carried on, "one of the men on the job, set me up. He wanted me to get fired. He put a little package of marijuana in my locker, right as he knew the supervisor was doing a search." Norman wiped his mouth with the back of his hand, swallowed, and said, "It was luck on my side that made me not get fired. Because in those days, having weed on the job was a very serious offence." Everyone murmured their surprise at his good fortune. "But it was really because my uncle worked for them for almost ten years at that time, and he was a good worker. That's really what saved me from going to jail."

Rose stopped him. "No Norman, it was purely the work of God. God and God alone was on your side."

"I know what you mean," Norman said, and smiled as if he fully understood what had transpired. "Because it was clearly a miracle that day, I tell you. So, I just tell my uncle to send me home, man." He sat back in the couch, in quiet reflection. "Just send me back to Jamaica."

Cynthia got up to turn on the ceiling light in the living room, and put on the lights around the house. Gurley cleared the glasses and bottles from the table, and took them to the kitchen.

Rose drew closer to Norman, admiring his courage to return to Jamaica to forge a living after knowing what it was like to live in Canada and earn Canadian dollars. "Boy, I was never happier to see Jamaica after that incident," Norman said.

75

Michelle Thompson

He told Rose that it had been thirty years since he had returned home with no regrets, nor the desire to return to Canada to stay; Rose was amazed by this. Everyone she knew who had come to Canada so far, had stayed, and wanted her to stay.

Rose became pensive, lots to think about now that the option to return home seemed a possibility. A sudden breeze fluttered the curtains next to her and drew her attention through the window. She gazed off into the darkening sky, thinking about Norman's lucky break. Things could have gone bad for him, but things worked out in his favour. Rose wondered if she went back to Jamaica, would she be as lucky as Norman, starting up her sewing business again, with God on her side. Realizing that the opposite could happen too, making her a failure, unable to help her family, Rose lamented, "Boy, this thing called life, we can never tell how it's going to turn out." She shook her head. "You don't know what to do."

"Life is a delicate dance, I tell you, but it's one we do every day, hoping for the best," Norman said.

Gurley came back to the room with pudding for everyone. She handed Rose a slice and said, "Come on, take this", Rose took the plate, "And stop your fretting."

Rose, speaking in a drawl as if just tired of the whole thing, said, "Life... life don't always set like rain, and when it pours, you just have to reach for shelter wherever you find it. Because life don't really care about nothing or nobody." She picked up her fork and started eating. The food, like heartbreak, went down hard, pushing past doubt, fear, even regret, resting in confusion. She put down her fork and pondered aloud: "Canada is not like Jamaica, where the sea wind blows hot and slow, and everything is, no problem, man! Here, it gets cold and snowy."

"And a lot of times, lonely," Norman inserted.

"Yet that never seemed to stop anyone from staying and making a living," she said, wondering if she had the will to try.

"Rose, you're worrying too much," Gurley said, taking her seat. "I know this wouldn't be a hard decision for me because I doubt very much, I could go back to Jamaica to live. For one, the Jamaican dollar don't worth anything. It's like play-play money these days. And I hear people can hardly get food in the supermarket."

"That's because nobody wants to plow the land, even the food them want from foreign," Norman said, shaking his head. "I'm one of a few productive farmers left down there."

"That's why America own Jamaica and we're tied up with this IMF," he said, adding, "you know what them call the IMF?" They waited. "It's Manley's fault." They all laughed, except for Rose, she was still lost in thought.

"But it's not just Manley's fault, it's Seaga's too. Both PNP and JLP have their fair share of the blame," Gurley said.

Cynthia, entering the room, added, "Politics mash-up Jamaica." Then she asked, "Norman, you want anything before you leave? Some coffee or tea?"

"No, me alright."

"Boy, I remember the good old days," Gurley said. "When the Jamaican dollar was stronger than the U.S. dollar, and people could live a decent life." She sighed. "I would have never left that little piece of paradise, Jamaica, if things didn't get so bad." She stretched and yawning, said, "I don't know what could make me go back there now."

Rose sat on the side listening, feeling low spirited by the negativity surrounding Jamaica's condition. But although she was vexed, she was calm. "Nobody would leave," she said, flatly, and excused herself from their company.

She entered the darkened room, leaving the light off. Rose dropped her body facedown in the bed, with the pillow over her head, as if holding her thoughts into place. With her face covered, she looked down a black hole of what-ifs and saw that the impossible trumped the possible. Not long after being in bed, her mind strayed to a car that had stopped at the gate. She heard Cynthia and Norman walking and talking along the porch near her bedroom. They said good night, and Norman went into the car, and it drove away. Cynthia came back inside the house and closed the door, her footsteps drew nearer and nearer to Rose's room. Cynthia knocked on her door and she pretended to be asleep. When the knocking stopped, she heard her bedroom door open. She kept still.

"Rose, you're sleeping?" Cynthia asked from the doorway, one hand on the knob, the other braced against the wall. She was determined to converse with Rose. Rose appreciated her not turning on the light. "Rose, how you gone to sleep already?" she joshed. Rose remained quiet, avoiding even a little banter with her friend. "Anyway, like I said, if you stay, I will do everything in my power to help you." Cynthia doubted Rose was asleep and continued, "Just try it for a few months, man. What you have to lose?" Rose fought to keep her hand at her side, and not brush the itch on her nose. "At least you will go home with a little money, which is better than nothing." She paused, hoping that Rose would acknowledge her, and in the silence, the phone rang. She went to her bedroom to answer it. Rose heard her having a friendly conversation with the caller before returning to her doorway. "Come Rose, the phone is for you. It's a call from Jamaica."

CHAPTER nine

It was two weeks and two days since Rose had left Jamaica on a three-week visitor's visa. She had been granted entry to Canada on the invitation of her best friend, Cynthia. Against the advice of her friend and everyone she had met so far in Canada, she should stay and try to make a living for her family in Jamaica, which meant putting her dream of wanting to sew for a living, on hold. Rose didn't yet make the decision that only she alone could make. However, the last time she spoke with her family, it was a call about the landlord's visit to notify them of a rent increase. Rose suspected it was because the landlord surmised that she had gone abroad, and like most Jamaicans with a visa to travel to North America, rarely returned prior to receiving their landed residency. She knew he would expect Canadian dollars to pour into 18A Summerfield Road from her. The pressure of the decision to stay or leave was made clear by the fact of the rent increase, as well as her mother's words: "Stay and work and save your little money; me and the children will manage". Even the children, although they missed their mother, were enjoying a little freedom from her strict, overprotectiveness. They too saw the financial advantages for the family. With her family on the side of her staying, she felt relieved; the decision to stay was made by the family.

Gurley and Cynthia congregated in Rose's room Thursday night, two days prior to the day of her original departure. They were happy for her. "Alright then Rose, Saturday I can carry you down to the agency that I started out with," Gurley told her.

"Saturday!" Cynthia exclaimed. "What about tomorrow?"

Cynthia eagerly wanted Rose to get started in a job to solidify her seriousness.

"Don't forget me have the people them work tomorrow, Cynthia. But the agency is open half-day on Saturdays, and me can speak to me Saturday boss that me coming in the afternoon."

Cynthia agreed that it was fine. "And if that don't work, you could take her on Monday," she insisted.

Rose sat on the edge of her bed listening as the women planned the next illegal steps of her life in Canada. As usual, they had no regard of her being delinquent in Canada, everybody did it, was the mind-set. To Rose's friends, it was the natural progression for individuals who got a chance to come abroad seeking a way to provide for themselves and their families.

Mrs. Pettipiece telephoned Cynthia and reported that Mr. Pettipiece did not have a discharge date yet, but she should be home soon. Cynthia planned a visit for her sick neighbour the next day. "Rose, follow me to the hospital tomorrow to look for Mr. P." Cynthia was not about to waste a day of her plans to get her friend a job as soon as she could, and the Pettipieces' were the obvious sure bet.

Approximately 10:15 a.m. Cynthia and Rose drove up to North York Centenary Hospital. She drove her inherited 1980 army-green Volvo, the car her husband Irv had left her, the one his daughters had wanted to sell after his death, which was not about to happen with Cynthia. Cynthia used to take her husband to his doctor's appointments in it, so not only was the car in good condition, it held special memories of them together. Cynthia drove to the underground ramp of the hospital, stopped at the entrance, and leaned outside to grab the ticket from the machine. "One thing I hate about coming to hospitals," she said, frowning, "it's the high cost of them parking ticket." Cynthia hissed as she pulled the ticket from the meter. "I don't know why it has to cost so much," she said, looking at the amount on the paper. Cynthia didn't have to struggle for money, but her Jewish husband, as she often said, taught her how to be thrifty.

Cynthia and Rose took the elevator up to the 4th floor, the intensive care unit. She went to the receptionist. "I'm here to see Mr. Pettipiece in room 409A." The receptionist told her to hold on while she called the room. Shortly after, Mrs. Pettipiece came to the front desk to greet Cynthia and Rose. She told the women that Mr. Pettipiece was just wheeled down to X-ray for a test, but that he should be returning soon. Cynthia told Mrs. Pettipiece that she would wait, as there was no need for her to rush home without seeing her old friend. After all, Cynthia wasn't about to let her parking ticket go to waste.

Cynthia and Rose went down to the lower-level cafeteria, and Mrs. Pettipiece waited in her husband's ICU room, for his return. The cafeteria was busy with mostly patients and their visitors. Cynthia and Rose spun around trying to find a table. They spotted an area with a few empty seats, but nearing the section, saw the sign STAFF ONLY. Just as they were about to exit the cafeteria, two women at a table next to them suggested the two extra seats at their table. Rose quickly held the seats at the four-seater table, while Cynthia went to purchase the coffee.

Rose nodded her greetings to the women. They looked around the same age as her, and when they started to speak, recognized that they too were Jamaicans. They all chuckled at this realization, and she shook hands with Doreen Mitchell and Monica Jenkins. The two women said they had been strangers until a couple of weeks ago when they had met each other, also in the cafeteria and had since become close. "I'm Rose," she said, hesitating to say her last name, but as the women stared at her, she told herself why worry, not only did she have one more legal day in the country, the women could also be in a similar position. "Tomlinson, my name is Rose Tomlinson."

"Tomlinson?" Monica said. "You know me know some Tomlinson in Manchester. Is Manchester you come from?"

"No, Tomlinson is my married name." Even discussing her last name felt off-putting to Rose, as she didn't want to open up about her marriage and subsequent divorce so quickly, and most of all that she was about to become a new escapee to Canada. Rose wished for Cynthia to hurry and join them, so she could help her to gage how much to say. She smiled a lot until Cynthia arrived at the table, carrying the two cups of coffee and muffins. Rose pulled out the chair for her to sit and drew her into their conversation. "This is my friend Cynthia. Cynthia, this is Doreen and Monica, they're also from Jamaica."

Rose told them that her and Cynthia were visiting Cynthia's neighbour in ICU, to which Doreen said, "My husband is in ICU too. He's there now going on two weeks." Rose enquired of Doreen what happened to her husband. Suddenly Doreen looked distraught before she said, "Boy it is so weird." She explained that her husband had only been in Canada not fully a week. He had come up for them to be married. She said the night of their honeymoon, when they were celebrating, he had a stroke in bed. Doreen looked shy when she said, "Right there on top of me, him heart give way." Monica chuckled. "No Monica it nuh funny. Because see him in ICU there, we not sure if him going to make it."

"And if you ever know the big bill him accumulate in this hospital without OHIP. Because I was supposed to sponsor him, but now I don't know if that can still happen with him being sick." Doreen took a big breath and said, "I don't know, we had so many plans for him to come up and get a job, and for us to buy a house. But now this happened." She shook her head and sighed heavily. "Boy, the situation not pretty, it not pretty at all."

Cynthia and Rose just sat there sipping their coffees, picking at their muffins, and nodded their empathy for the woman.

Monica said her mother had been in intensive care too, but had got a little better and had been recently transferred to a medical floor. "And the doctor said it looks like she will need an operation." Rose ears perked up when Monica started talking about her mother, and she asked what happened. "The doctor diagnosed my mother with stage four kidney disease."

"It's a serious thing. And a lot of our people have trouble with the diabetes that brings on the kidney disease," Cynthia said.

"They will have to cut off one or probably both of her legs, the doctors said. And she already losing her eyesight because of the diabetes."

Rose gasped when she heard this. "How old is your mother?" she asked. Monica said seventy-nine and Rose quickly thought of her mother at seventy-four, and was glad she had had no diagnosis of diabetes. Still, Rose's heart quieted a little.

"Diabetes is a curse of many Jamaicans," Cynthia said.

Cynthia told the women that her neighbour might be discharged from intensive care if the test he took today proves negative.

"Oh Lord." Doreen rested her hand at her jaw. "I don't even know when my husband going to leave hospital. Him just open his eyes this morning, and he's still not talking. Him paralyze on the right side, and it affect him speech. The doctors talking about sending him to rehab."

"That would be good if he gets rehabilitation," Cynthia said. "My husband, before he died, had a stroke that affected his walking, it was just a T.I., a mini-stroke, but he went to rehab and improved a whole lot."

"Ah, my dear, my husband not that fortunate. You don't hear the worse, he doesn't have health insurance. The insurance that he came to Canada with is no good here, only in Jamaica. And I never started filling his landed papers yet because the stroke happened on our wedding night."

"And I'm not sure like how the two of you weren't married before he came up, and the papers weren't filed, I don't know if he would qualify for OHIP because of you," Cynthia said.

"What about regular insurance?" Rose asked.

"All I have is my OHIP and as I said, his insurance not good here. All those things were going to get looked about, but this happened," Doreen lamented. "Insurance not cheap. So, I don't know how he's going to manage, because he can't go to rehab without some sort of insurance to cover it, or able to pay out of pocket, which we don't have."

"Boy, you certainly in a pickle," Cynthia said. "All you can do now is pray."

"You certainly right, that's all I can do. That's all I've been doing."

"Hey, by the way, any of you ladies know about any days work for someone who don't have them papers yet?" The women looked at each other and said they did not know of anyone. Both women had their Canadian landed papers. Doreen worked in a hotel and Monica worked in a factory. However, Monica said her mother worked with a man over a year ago in his home but was unable to continue due to her recurring illness, and that he didn't have anybody steady helping him.

"Which one of you looking for work?" Monica asked. Cynthia pointed to Rose, who sheepishly acknowledged it was she. "I could talk to him for you." Cynthia said it would be kind and asked where he lived. "Him name Nico Barros, and he lives around Eglinton and Oakwood area."

Cynthia told Rose, "That is not far from me."

"Yeah man, I could talk to him because since my mother left him last year, he doesn't have no steady person. I go and help him sometimes."

"About how old him is?" Rose asked, trying to measure the weight of the work, should something work out.

"Him not that old you know, he's about seventy-one. It's just that him had a stroke a few years ago that leave him left hand not functioning." Rose asked for specifics. "Him walk with a limp and use a cane, and as I said, the left hand not working at all. He basically needed somebody to cook — sometimes, because he eats out a lot, and to clean up the house and wash for him." Rose and Cynthia looked at each other and nodded their heads in agreement that it was doable. "Oh, and him is a pensioner, and him pay alright. So, if you want, I'll speak with him and if he says yes, take you to his house."

Cynthia asked, "How soon this can happen?"

Monica said, "By Monday or so, because I'm on sick leave now taking care of my mother. So, when I come to visit her, you can meet me here, and I will take you to Nico. It's not that far from here."

Cynthia, keeping track of the time to go back to Mr. Pettipiece's room, wished the women well and got up to leave. "Doreen, I pray things work out for you and your husband," she said.

By the time Cynthia and Rose went back to Mr. Pettipiece's room, he had returned but was asleep, weary from all the tests.

Mrs. Pettipiece said, "We should get the results by tomorrow, I suppose, and we'll know when he gets to come home."

Under fifteen minutes of leaving the hospital, Cynthia and Rose were back at home. Cynthia went to the kitchen to start dinner and Rose joined her there. She wasted no time. "Well, Rose, lots to think about. See things already looking up. You go and meet with this man Monday and I'm sure he'll like you." Rose reminded her that Gurley was to take her to the agency.

"Don't you see that this is a sure thing right now. And with the agency you will have to give them something out of your money, don't think it's for free. You'll have to pay them to get you work, also you have no choice in the matter of who or where you will work. But with this man, you already have an idea about him, and the pay will go straight into your pocket and straight towards your family at home."

Rose nodded pensively, thinking of the possibilities.

CHAPTER Ten

Monday morning, Cynthia dropped Rose at the hospital to meet Monica. Monica waited downstairs near the exit for Rose and Rose transferred into her car. "I only have about an hour," Monica said, driving out of the hospital. "I like to be there when my mother gets her medication, uhm, you never know, sometimes them nurses could be tired. I don't want them giving her wrong meds, so I like to be there if I can." Rose listened as Monica spoke; she could tell that Monica cared as much for her mother as she did hers. "Not to worry, we can get to Nico and back by then," Monica assured her.

Monica parked in front of Nico's bungalow. The house was much smaller than Cynthia's and much less tidy in the front yard. There was a black Pinto parked at the side of the house. It had dust all over it, as if he hadn't driven it since his stroke. Rose walked behind Monica to Nico's front door. Beer cans piled up in the veranda corner; a cigarette box, and a lighter with an ash tray were on the floor next to a chair. Rose took into consideration that Nico was not working with all his physical capabilities. *Lord, it looks like me will have me work cut out for me.*

"Him live alone? I mean, him have any family?" Rose whispered to Monica at the door.

"From I know Nico," Monica whispered back, "And that is going on five years now, I have never seen him with any family. Him usually by himself or with him friends down at the corner coffee shop."

Monica knocked on the door. A raspy voice from inside answered, "Come in." They entered Nico's equally scraggly living room, no different from the yard. He sat in his lounge chair wearing his sleeveless undershirt and boxing shorts, drinking a beer. "Welcome ladies. Have a seat."

Rose looked around the room and saw some semblance of chairs, but they all had either a piece of clothing or newspaper on them. Rose told Nico thanks but no thanks as she did not think they were staying. Monica disregarded his invitation to sit and got to the point. "Nico, this is the lady I told you about, Rose. She can help you cleanup around the house, even the yard if you want." Rose cleared her throat to stop Monica at "even the yard", but knew that if she were to seriously consider the job, it would include the yard and everything Nico needed done, within reason.

"Nice to meet you Rose, hope you're here to stay." Nico chuckled. "The last girl I had didn't last a week. I hope you last at least a week and a half." Nico's hoarse, cigarette laughter bellowed through the room. Rose was quickly realizing that Nico loved to laugh at other people's expense, and at his own jokes. She slanted her mouth in a fake smile.

"So, Nico, I can't stay long, are you interested in Rose or what?"

"Well, if she is interested in me." He swayed his hand side by side. "Look at me, if she can handle me, and not run home crying, I'm hiring. And I pay well too." Then he mumbled sarcastically, "Don't know why the others ran off", and laughed again. Rose ignored his incessant laughter and enquired about the pay. "More than most people would pay." Nico was a retired engineer with the Canadian National Railway, and he was before that, in the Canadian Armed Forces. He received a handsome pension for both. "Is $150 enough for the week? And you won't have to work on weekends either. How's that for employer of the year, even better, employer of the century." Nico cracked himself up laughing. Rose wished Cynthia was there to discuss the pay, but she figured that amount was a hundred and fifty more than she had. She asked when he wanted her to start, a question that was more of a stalling tactic, because in that moment, she wished that she didn't even have to consider a job with Nico. But Cynthia was home waiting to hear nothing other than – hired! As well, her family was depending on her. "Again, I say, if you can start right away, that works for me." He pushed himself up with his one good hand from the chair. "Let me show you around," he said.

Rose followed him while Monica remained standing in the living room. Nico took Rose to the bedroom first. "I'm hardly in here, I sleep on the sofa in the living room." Rose noticed that although Nico did not sleep in his bedroom, it was just as untidy as if he did. "This is the bathroom," he said, pushing the door opened for her to see inside. The stench of urine permeated the bathroom, and the smell spilled into the hallway. Rose held her breath as she went by. Nico continued the tour by showing Rose the second bedroom; it doubled as a storage room of old newspapers and canned and packed goods. "You don't have to bother with this room, it's organized chaos," he told her with his signature scruffy laughter.

They got to the back of the house and passing a closed door, Rose asked, "What's in this room?"

"Oh, it's my laundry room." He opened it, and Rose almost regretted asking, but it would soon be a room she would need to go into anyway. Clothes and bed linens were all over the place, in multiple baskets, soiled and seemingly clean mixed together. Rose closed her eyes, held her breath for a couple of seconds, and acknowledged the Lord: *Help me father, God*.

Rose could have started work the same day, but wanted to go home to process the mess she was setting to embark on. Monica took Rose all the way home since she had some time, instead of having Cynthia pick her up at the hospital.

"Thank you, Monica, I appreciate you doing this," Cynthia said to Monica at the gate. "Call me anytime."

Cynthia and Rose waved at Monica driving off and as they entered the home, Cynthia said, "So how it went today Rose, you taking the work?"

CHAPTER Eleven

On Monday morning, three days after accepting Nico's job, Rose took two short bus rides and in under thirty minutes, she was at his house for 9 a.m. Nico had told her that he wasn't an early riser, so not to come before ten o'clock. Rose wanted to get in and out of Nico's home, get her work done and go home, so she reasoned him down for her to begin at nine o'clock.

Nico slept in the sofa and was there to open the door at the first knock. He had made some coffee and offered Rose some. "Help yourself," he told her, raising his cup to her. "I made a pot." Rose was not ready to eat at Nico's home and told him that she had already had her first cup and only drank one cup of coffee in the morning. This fib she felt sorry for telling but looking around Nico's house, she didn't think he would appreciate the truth.

"I better get to it Mr. Nico because there is plenty to do." Rose observed the unkempt living room, trying to keep the disgust off her face.

"What do you think, girl, I'm a slave driver? Sit and take a rest, you just got here." Girl, didn't sit well with Rose, but she chucked it off as Nico being an old fool that paid well.

"No sir, it's best to start early, get most things done and be out of the way." Rose repeated that there was really plenty to do. "And if you don't mind, if I get my work done early, I'd like to leave early sir."

"Who you are calling sir?" Nico asked, laughing. "Sir is for my father. I'm plain, old Nico Barros, Nico for you, pretty lady." Rose forced a smile and excused herself to go and change in the bathroom.

The first thing Rose did after changing into work clothes was put on the pair of rubber gloves she brought. Under the bathroom sink was the cleaning implements, and she tackled there first, beginning with the badly discoloured toilet bowl, and then the equally grimy bathtub. She not only started with the bathroom because she was standing there, but there was no way, she told herself, that she could have gone to the toilet in the condition it was. Scrubbing and disinfecting, she wondered how long the bathroom had gotten a proper cleaning. It was no wonder no helper wanted to stay. Finished, she stepped back to examine the bathroom and was pleased with her handiwork, which gave her vigour and confidence to challenge the rest of the house.

Onto the kitchen next, Rose intended. As she opened the bathroom door, Nico was in front of the door with the silliest grin. He startled her, and she stuttered, "Mr. Barros, sir, sorry, sir", casting her eyes downward and away from his stare. Rose wasn't sure what to make of her new boss standing quietly outside the bathroom. *Was he there to deliberately scare me or what?*

"Finally," he said when she opened the door. "I thought you weren't coming out today." Looking sheepishly, his both hands cupping his manly parts, he said, "I've been standing here holding my piss, little lady."

He twisted on the spot like a child in potty-training. Rose thought it a little off that Nico needed the bathroom as she was in there, and although she tried to dismiss the thought that he might be up to no good, his glances wouldn't let her think otherwise. It was a look her mind confirmed that he was up to no good. "Sorry sir," she said again, trying to go by him to the kitchen.

To Rose's surprise and dismay, her mind was not fooling her, because as she tried to scoot past Nico, he slapped after her buttocks. "Come here lily gal," he said, and laughed as if Rose had given him permission to act in that manner with her.

Rose was caught off guard by Nico's actions. She quickly dodged his hand and carried on to the kitchen. Flabbergasted, she stood in the kitchen catching her breath, wondering what had just happened. *Is this man crazy?* It took her a moment to compose herself. She looked around the kitchen trying to figure out where to begin with the many bags of groceries, canned goods, food flies swarming containers of stale dinners, and cat food laid out on the counter. Cat food? She picked up one of the small cans. *I never know him have cat?* The things that were not good were mixed in with what were usable. She hesitated to go and ask Nico what to throw out and what to keep for fear of more of his antics, when he came into the kitchen. "I was just about to come ask how you want me to sort these groceries and things, Mr. Nico?" He said everything should be kept until she pointed out the old food gathering flies.

"That can go in the fridge. I'll warm it up for supper." Rose offered to cook some fresh food and he said, "Let's finish that first, there's still plenty to eat there."

Rose asked about the food on the counter, which were more than could hold in the cupboard. "Why don't you take some and send them for your children back home?"

"That's kind but no thanks, sir, I haven't started to pack a barrel as yet." Rose had read the labels and saw that the date for most of the canned foods had long expired. But Nico insisted. "You can't throw out food, especially when others can eat it." Rose had to tell him that most had expired.

"Don't watch the dates, that's just the date they put on stuff so you run out and buy more."

"I didn't know you had a cat?"

"My cat Tiger went missing. I keep his food in case he comes back."

Nico explained that his cat liked to go wandering around the neighbourhood and one day he never came back. "It's almost a year now but I keep hoping." Rose saw a bit of sorrow come over Nico and urged him to get another cat. "No other could replace Tiger." She felt empathy for Nico, seeing him with new eyes, until he said, "Maybe you'll let me pat your little behind the way I patted his", followed by his annoying laughter that turned Rose's stomach.

Rose frowned. "Mr. Nico, I don't like the way you talk to me, sir," she said. "It's not nice."

"Ah, I'm just playing with you."

"I don't play like that, sir, I'm a married woman." Rose found herself lying to keep Nico at bay, but that was for nought.

He told her that he did not see a wedding ring on her finger and thought she was "a nice-looking gal", to which Rose frowned in disgust.

"Me not wearing a ring doesn't say anything, sir, I just don't like to wear it when I'm at work." She picked up a couple of the canned beans and began packing them in the overhead cupboard. "If you don't mind sir, I'll like to do my work."

For the rest of the morning Rose worked like a robot, keeping out of Nico's way, only speaking to him when necessary. She watched the clock and counted the minutes. And when he got dressed to go and meet his friends at the coffee shop, she welcomed his absence. "I'll soon be back, little lady, need anything, a donut or a sandwich?"

"No sir, you take your time." As soon as Nico had left, Rose called Cynthia. "Me say girl, not even you could stomach this mess me deal with today, just to keep a job." Rose joined Cynthia in a hearty laughter. "Me say, the man nasty and messy, is a shame, no wonder nobody nuh stay with him. And another thing too, him so darn fresh, a call big woman gal and little lady, and it's two time him lick after me bottom today."

"What? A fresh him fresh," Cynthia said. "If him ever try that again, tell him you will have to bring your husband down there to have a word with him." The two women burst out laughing.

"Ah Cynthia, poor Arthur. If him was even in my life, him couldn't stand to have a word with anyone, much less fling a punch after them. The drunken fart him is," Rose said. But a sudden sadness came over her for her ex-husband, and her chest heaved slightly. "May God help him."

She wrapped up the call with Cynthia and went to check on the laundry. The coloured ones were finished, and the badly discoloured white ones were soaking. She swept and wiped the veranda, threw out the trash, putting the empty beer cans and bottles in a separate bag for return. Nico returned around 3 p.m. and released her to go after she had completed the duties. "Anything else you want me to do for the day, sir?" Rose asked once the house was cleaned and the laundry was done. Nico had nothing more for her to do and she bid him "goodbye, sir."

"See you tomorrow, lil gal."

Rose could hear his laughter trailing her. She was so happy to be over her first day at Nico's that she couldn't bother to take him on. She simply faked a smile of acknowledgement and hurried to catch her bus.

Cynthia met Rose at the door as Rose entered the home, excited for Rose. "Rosie," Cynthia said, calling her affectionately.

She was pleased with Rose. "You did it girl, see, you can do it!" She embraced Rose, and Rose, feeling tired, barely raised her hand, but grinned proudly of her accomplishment. Cynthia said, sort of jokingly, "So, did you put that man Nico in his place today?"

"Cynthia, me say, I had to stand up strong as not to quit on my first day. That man, he is something else," Rose said with scorn. She hung her purse and the light jacket she wore in the closet. Frustratingly, she continued, "Now I know why all the workers that come to work for him don't stay." However frustrated Rose was, she knew in a more acceptable situation, working with Nico would have been a dream, a job with great pay, and overall, not very demanding. *I guess you can't have it all*, she summed up her reality.

"Come sit down, my love. As a matter of fact, the dinner ready, might as well come eat."

"Let me take a quick shower first, Cynthia."

Afterwards, Rose joined Cynthia in the kitchen; she set the table for her and Cynthia. "Gurley home yet?" Cynthia reminded her that Gurley had a few more hours before she got home. She shared dinner for both of them and sat at the table. "So give me a run-down of the day. But eat first."

Rose told her everything about Nico's crude behaviour and his messy place, she even told her about his missing cat. "But you know," Rose said, thoughtfully. "I feel that cat is dead, but Mr. Nico holding on to the possibility that the cat is still alive and will come back. He feels that he is going to see the cat show up one day at his doorstep."

Cynthia, sitting across from Rose at the table, said, "Or maybe he knows that the cat is dead but holding on to the memory gives him comfort. Because if you say he doesn't have any family, the cat might be it for him. Poor thing," Cynthia said, showing genuine concern. "I feel sorry for him, God know."

The women ate quietly for a moment until Rose said, "That's why me never walk off the job today you know, me see that him lonely, and him want company, him must want a woman." Rose noticed Cynthia setting to laugh, so she added, "But it's not me."

"You sure?" Cynthia teased.

"Very much so," Rose answered, trying not to laugh with Cynthia, who couldn't hold back her laughter. "And if me have to resurrect the marriage with me and Arthur, just to keep him off my back— "

"Literally off your back my dear," Cynthia further teased, cracking herself up.

Rose continued, "Then that is what I will have to do. Because those dirty fingernails that me see on Mr. Nico, and his clothes is always a shamble." Rose made a disgusting face. "Come to think of it, I never really seen him in the bathroom bathing, unless it's after I leave."

"Maybe him need help bathing," Cynthia said.

"As a matter of fact, me offer to set the tub of water for him, and of course him have to run him slack joke, 'you gonna come in the tub with me', he said, with him creepy self." Rose shook her head and continued eating.

"Then who tell you him joking," Cynthia said. "Him well serious."

"Well, if him serious, him will have to stay dirty, for all I know. There is no way on God's great earth I could consider a man like him." As if she just remembered, "And the more him call me lil gal, baby girl, little lady, and try to touch me, is the more him sicken me."

Cynthia finished eating and pushed her plate aside. "Well, you doing as best you can, cleaning up after him. God will bless you for that, for sticking with him."

"For now," Rose quickly added.

"For now, yes, nothing not carved in stone. No contract was signed. Just look at it as one hand wash the other, right? You help him stay clean and cook the occasional meal for him, and him pay you so you have money to buy things to send to you family, medicine for your mother. Fair and square, nothing wrong with that."

Rose attempted to say more, but the words got trapped in hesitation.

Cynthia picked up on Rose's reluctance and wondered what she was hiding. "What's wrong Rose? You have something to say?"

Rose was sitting on a ton of emotions to keep from exploding. Cynthia wouldn't let up because she saw that whatever it was, it clearly vexed her friend. "Rose," Cynthia perplexed, called out. "What's the matter?"

"It's Nico. I don't think I'm the helper for him."

"What you mean? You're not looking for marriage with him. Him pay well and that's all you need from him."

"The truth is, him is a nasty, dirty man," Rose said, frowning. "Two times today him walk past me stark naked, no decency toward me."

"How you mean, Rose? Naked, naked, without any clothes on?" Cynthia's eyes bulged.

"Yes, you don't hear me, naked! Naked as the day him born. Him little nook a jiggle up and down." Cynthia couldn't unsee the picture in her head and laughed out loud. "You don't see that the man is just slack and nasty?"

"Me a try imagine him."

"No, you don't want to imagine that."

"Well, he's certainly a dirty bastard for sure," Cynthia said and rolled her eyes.

"And all now him not looking at me, but I know he wants me to see him. Him come right up before me like him picking up something off the floor. I pretend not to see him though."

"Oh Lord!"

"Boy, me a tell you Cynthia, eye water come to my eyes, me had to lock myself in the bathroom for a minute and catch my breath."

"Rose, me sorry to hear this. The hell we have to go through in this country, the things we have to put up with, just to get ahead in life."

"It sad, me tell you."

"Just for a better life," Cynthia lamented.

"But me not desperate. I tell you, I almost take my bag and come home. Just walk off the job." Rose shook her head slowly, reflectively. "Me say, if it wasn't for them four pickney and my mother, me would be on the plane back to Jamaica already."

"My child, never mind, this is not forever, God not sleeping," Cynthia consoled. "If him ever do it again, just tell him that you will walk off the job. That might smarten him up. Because him probably can't afford to lose another helper."

The women were quiet for a moment as Rose gathered her emotions and calmed herself.

Cynthia broke their silence. "By the way, this is a horse of different colour, but you know who called for you earlier on today?" Rose narrowed her brows. "Roy," Cynthia said, her smiling face signaled her approval.

Somehow shifting from Nico to Roy wasn't so bad for Rose because she had been thinking about him as someone to know now that she had planned to stay in Canada. She was ready to try new things and having someone who was not new to the country, someone other than Cynthia and Gurley, to communicate with and take her out, would be a worthy friend. "He asked that you give him a call."

"I don't even know where to find Roy's number now."

"I have it, he gave it to me in case you misplaced it," Cynthia said, and went to get the pad she had written it on. "Here, call him man, you need a little cheering up." She handed Rose the pad that she had written Roy's telephone number on. "Maybe old Nico sense that you could use some loving in your life," Cynthia said, making fun.

"Cynthia!" Rose shouted. "I can't even joke 'bout Nico right now. Ol' fart."

"No, but seriously, me and Roy was talking and him seem to not be a bad person at all. And him really seem to check for you." Rose looked at the phone number. "Call him, man," Cynthia urged.

Although tired, Rose figured she would give Roy a call at that moment; he had been trying to reach her from before Yvonne left. She went to the living room and this time took a seat by the phone. "Hello," she said when he answered, "Is this—?"

"Rose, yes, this is me, Roy." Rose asked how he knew it was her. "I remember your voice like it was yesterday. I can't forget you Rose." Rose's heart was touched, and she didn't know how to proceed with the softness forming in her heart. "I think about you all the time you know, and I've tried to reach you before." Rose remained quiet, not knowing how to respond to a man she barely knew fawning over her. It had been a long time since she was single. Her husband was all she had known for the last twenty years. Meeting someone interested in her at the beginning stages of her stay in Toronto was the last thing on her mind. She brushed it off, thinking the experience was too new and not to put any weight on it. There was a newness in her since she had decided to remain in Canada. Something inside her suddenly wanted to open up, live a little, and that quiet voice inside her urged, let him in. Cynthia seemed to like him and Yvonne had vouched for him.

Rose said to Roy, "Sorry that I don't share the same feelings for you Roy, the truth is that I don't know you."

"Just give me a chance to show you who I am and what I'm about."

"So, you have a wife or girlfriend?" Rose asked Roy. Roy laughed, and she said, insisting, "No, don't laugh, this is a serious question. I wouldn't want to start anything under false pretense."

"Rose if I were a married man would I be calling you?"

"Roy, please," Rose said and hissed. "Trust me Roy, men do these things all the time, this is not strange. And sad to say Jamaican men known for having a sweetheart with them wife."

"Well, that is not me, Rose."

"So how come you don't have a wife or girlfriend?" Rose persisted. "Every man, especially a good one, have a woman. Because women always want good man."

"To tell the truth, Rose —"

Rose interrupted, "Is the truth I want to hear, nothing but the truth."

"My wife died four years ago, and I haven't met anyone like her so far. She was my first and only true love. We have two grown children, two boys."

"Roy, that is a lot of pressure for any woman to live up to, the memory of a man's dead wife…his only true love," Rose said.

"No Rose, I like what I see so far, so you wouldn't have much to live up to. Just let me invite you out so you can see and learn more about me. I can't wait to know you better." Rose told him that she had a new job but was free on the weekend. Roy congratulated her on her new job, and all that she would be able to accomplish going forward. He suggested as a way of celebration, they go out Saturday night for dinner, just to have a drink and talk. "How do you feel about that?" Roy asked.

"As long as it's not Pepper Pot."

"No man, since that last incident when we were there, it got very slow, hardly anyone wants to go there anymore. I have a nice place to take you Rose, don't worry."

Roy and Rose planned an outing for Saturday night at a restaurant in the Eastend. Her talk with Roy lifted her spirits and took her mind off Nico for the moment.

For the rest of the week, Rose kept her 9 a.m. to 3 p.m. schedule with Nico. She came to realize that Nico took his evening nap around 3 p.m. and that was the reason why he had her leave at that time. That was fine with Rose, as she recognized that she would beat the traffic going home, and the school children leaving school at 3:30 p.m. Isn't God good, she told herself.

On Friday, Rose was happy to finish her first week. Since she would be gone for the weekend, she made sure all her chores were completed by 2:45 p.m., and she prepared to leave once Nico had come home at 3 o'clock. Rose noticed that 3:15 her employer had not arrived, 3:30 he still had not come home. She got a bit worried as he had always been home 3:10 the latest.

She thought of going down to the coffee shop but didn't want to miss him should he come home when she wasn't there. 4:30, 5:00, and still no Nico. Rose was genuinely concerned for her employer. She thought about Nico's health, that he had had a previous stroke and his smoking, not eating properly and not taking his medication as he should, could bring on another. The weak feeling in her stomach sped up, and she felt a headache coming on. By this time, she had been corresponding with Cynthia and the two were trying to decipher where Nico could be. Cynthia advised Rose to go to the coffee shop and enquire of him and if he was not there, for her to call the police; that was before she remembered that Rose couldn't have any tangling with the police. Going to the hospital, the women concluded, was the safest.

Rose went to the corner café and saw two young women behind the counter. Rose stood before the short-haired brunette who was busy rubbing off coffee and tea stains from the counter. Rose watched the girl for about a minute, until she looked up. "May I help you with something?" she asked, and listed off the specials they had for the day, without giving Rose a chance to say why she was there.

She spoke so quickly that Rose couldn't fully catch her words. The Canadian-English was still new to her, and instantly she became aware of her own speech and Jamaican accent.

"Ahm," she said. "I looking for a man name Mr. Barros."

The girl looked puzzled at Rose, as if she didn't understand her and she repeated herself. Rose felt awkward and embarrassed and sensitive about her Jamaican accent, and wanted to leave the coffee shop. What was even worse was that time was running out. It was close to 6 p.m. and she hadn't located her employer. The girl at the other end of the counter overhearing the conversation with Rose and her colleague came over, and said, "Are you looking for Nico?"

Rose was relieved that she might finally have gotten somewhere. "You know him, you know Mr. Nico?"

"Yes, there was an accident here today and—"

"And, and what? What happen? Mr. Nico ok, him okay?"

The girl wanted to know who Rose was, what was her relation to Nico. Rose explained that she had recently started to work for Nico and was expecting him home around 3 p.m.

"One of the men that Nico hangs out with here, he had a cardiac arrest and was taken to the hospital."

"Nico? Not Nico, right?"

"No, not Nico, but he went with his friend, actually he insisted that they take him in the ambulance." The young server told Rose that about six men have been meeting at the café for many years, they were like brothers, and for a couple of them, these were the only family they had.

"So which hospital him is?" The girl told Rose that the sick man was taken to North York Centenary Hospital and admitted to the ICU. She had spoken to Nico twenty minutes before Rose had come and he said that his friend had awakened and was doing better, but would be in hospital for a few days. "He said he was on his way home," the girl said. Rose's heart was relieved. She thanked the young server and went back to Nico's home.

Nico was home when she got there. "Oh Mr. Nico, I was worried bad for you. I thought something happen to you sir." Rose put her hand on her chest. "I was so worried. Thank God."

"It wasn't me who had the heart attack, it was my friend, but he's looking better now."

"That's what they told me at the coffee shop. I am so glad that you are okay sir," Rose said, smiling. "You want anything before I leave?"

"No, I'm good." Nico took his wallet from his pocket. "I want you to take a cab home."

"I can take the bus home sir, it's not that late." Rose looked at her watch. "It's only 6:40."

"No, I insist, for all I put you through, take this." He took five dollars from his wallet and gave it to Rose. "Here, take this for a cab home. As a matter of fact, let me call one right now."

After he called the cab, he said, "Don't let me forget your pay." He went to his bedroom and returned with $150 in an envelope and handed it to Rose. "You did good this week."

Rose reached home in ten minutes, and although she was hungry, she was more tired. She went to the bathroom before going to the kitchen against Cynthia's call to come and have a plate of the Friday evening special: pumpkin seasoned rice. Cynthia knew that Rose did not eat at Nico's, after having a full breakfast, she only took with her a yogurt and a couple of fruits to last the day. Being drained from the first work week, and especially the last few hours of Nico's disappearance, Rose had worked up an appetite, and had dinner while bringing Cynthia up to speed. Cynthia informed her that Audrey had called not too long before she came, to say that they got their phone lines today. Although Rose was excited that her family finally had a telephone, she was tired and preferred to get a little rest before calling. She remembered Roy wanted her to call him as well, to set a time for their date the following day.

Rose's rest turned into sleep and she never woke up until in the morning. Her first priority of the day was calling home, Roy could wait until after. She imagined her mother and the children waiting by the phone. Audrey screamed, "Mommy!" and her siblings came running. "Mommy is on the phone, one of you go get granny." The excitement from their congratulations on surviving her first employed week, gaining a salary that would allow her to start packing a barrel for them for Christmas, was the lift her life needed. All the children had a short conversation that echoed each other: they missed her and were putting their own list together for what they wanted at Christmas. She saved her mother for last. The children ran off when their grandmother took the phone. Her mother cried with joy for her. "Girl, I know it's hard to leave them children, but you doing the best thing; work your little money, that will benefit everybody."

"So how you doing Mama?"

"Me not doing too bad, and the children alright. Although Donovon will have to get him eyes tested, him need glasses. Him have to sit close up to the TV and him having headaches every day. And I feel it's because him straining him eyes."

Rose said she would send extra money to take care of the eye test and the glasses.

As soon as she came off the phone, Rose went to Cynthia to ask her if she had the time to take her to purchase a barrel and to do some shopping.

"Did you make a list? You don't want to go out there without a plan and waste time."

"I kind of have a list in my mind, because I know what they want."

"I still say make a list, write it down. As a matter of fact, you don't have to start shopping now, you have months to pack a barrel. If you're on the street and see something you know they'll need, then buy it." Rose shook her head in agreement. "And you have to get a barrel, and transportation to bring it home, because my car can't carry it." Rose wracked her brain to quickly come up with ways to get a van or a truck. "Really Rose, you don't have to rush it. When do you want to send the barrel?" Rose told her for Christmas. "So, you can start packing at least two months before because you have to give time for shipment. As you see something they need, you buy." Rose accepted Cynthia's reasoning.

Rose forgot to call Roy to confirm what time he would pick her up. She got carried away in assisting Cynthia to tidy up and do the laundry. When he didn't hear from her around midday, he called her. "Oh Roy, sorry but I forgot, man. My family got their phone yesterday and we spoke this morning, and our talk still on my mind so much, I forgot everything else." Rose told him that she would need a truck or van to pick up the barrel. "Don't worry your head Rose, when the time comes, I can get transportation for you." Rose was elated by Roy's offer; one problem was solved. "Rose I'm happy for you, truly happy that things working out," Roy said. "So, what about later? We should go out and celebrate, man."

"To be honest Roy, I am not ready. I'm sorry."

"You're not ready Rose? All we'd be doing is going for a bite."

"Yes, but not tonight, I am really tired. This first week of work drained me. Let's choose another time."

"And next time you'll say, another time. Then what about tomorrow?" Roy said.

"No, man," she replied. She could sense Roy's frustration through the phone. "Let's see what next weekend brings, okay?"

Roy realized Rose had slipped back into her old ways with him, and said, "Alright Rose, I hear you." Feeling doubtful of future chances, he said, "Okay, if you say so. We can see how next week, or even another time." And sounding dejected he added, "Get your rest." It continued like this for weeks. Roy continued to pursue Rose to no avail.

Rose had gotten into a routine at Nico, and apart from his continuous "freshness", she tolerated working with him because the work was not heavy, and she handled his flirting by just ignoring him. On top of that, and most importantly, the pay afforded her the things her family needed. The children expected a barrel for Christmas, and welcomed money in a letter each month; those things were her concern for the moment. It wasn't only Donovan who needed glasses, they all needed their eyes tested, her mother told her, and there were the occasional school trips. Rose's money even went to help Arthur, when he got sick. The children called her urgently one day to say that they had gone to visit their father and he was home in bed, roasting with fever and looking poorly. "He doesn't look good, Mommy. I think he should go to the doctor," Maureen, her middle daughter and her father's ardent advocate had said. She was the child whom he seemed to favour, maybe because as he said, she resembled his mother.

"Maureen! Where you think me must find money for your father to go doctor? Him should think 'bout these things happening to him when him reaching for the rum bottle." But as much as she was disgusted with Arthur and his drinking, hearing the pain in her children's voices for their father was hard for her to take. "Did he feel sorry for me when him use to bust my behind? When him did a choke me to death?" She teared up as her emotions grew, yet after she calmed herself, she'd say, "Alright, let me see what I can come up with." The children would cheer her on, to which she would say, "But this is the last time. I don't want to have nothing to do with that man, not even to save him life." It was not the first nor the last time, and on every occasion that her children called pleading for help for their father, her heart relented, and she felt better for helping.

A few months into working with Nico, Rose noticed that he was receiving regular correspondence. He would speak on the phone to someone that sounded like he was speaking to a relative, and he received letters he would leave on the center table unopened. Rose had to dust the table with the letters on it, and they had started piling up, so she neatly stacked them to the side. In handling the letters, she realized they came from the same person, Tony Barros, at the same stamped address, North Ontario Correctional Centre. *Correctional centre? As in jail?* Her interest peaked, however, she felt she could never dare to ask Nico for fear of seeming nosey. But she found another way of satisfying her curiosity.

One day, after clearing the mailbox, Rose took the mail to Nico. He was sitting in his lounge chair with his feet stretched out on the table, next to the pile of older letters. "Mr. Nico, you got a letter, sir." Nico leaned to get the letter from Rose and his feet knocked off the letters next to him. Rose picked them up, "Oh, oh," she said as she stooped to pick them up. Observing them in front of Nico, she said, "And look, sir, all of them coming from the same person, a Tony Barros." Smiling, and pretending to be innocent, she asked, "Your relative sir?"

Nico took the letter and stuttered, "Yeah, yes", as if ashamed to say so.

"I notice a few more piling up there," she said and pointed to the ones that had fallen off the table. "You want me to get your glasses sir?" He told her to get his glasses from his room. Rose returned with his bifocals.

Nico read the letter. "Goddamn it!" he said, and flung the letter across the room. He used his foot to brush the others off the table. "Goddamn imbecile!" he said. Rose enquired what was wrong. "That stupid nephew of mine, went and got himself in trouble."

Rose gasped and asked, "Is what him do sir?"

"He and his friend got caught breaking and entering." Nico frowned. "Stupid bastard. And now his mother is asking me to help him out." Rose asked how. "He needs a place to stay when he gets out of jail." Rose realized that it was Nico's sister who had been calling and they sometimes got into heated conversations.

"So, what about his mother? Him can't stay with her?"

"My sister moved out to Alberta, and he doesn't want to go there. And now she wants me to help him when he gets out, until he finds work or decide to go to her."

"So, about when him would come out?"

"Next week, by the look of it." Nico was upset, and fumed, "I mean the boy is nineteen, and you think he'd have some sense of responsibility. But no, no interest in going to college, just want to hang around the worst company and smoke drugs. My sister has tried so much with him, and yet he lets her down. I wouldn't be doing this if it wasn't for her."

Rose stayed quiet and let Nico vent; when he calmed down, she said, "You want me to do anything to prepare for him coming?"

"Ah, nothing at this point," Nico grumbled. "I'll just let him stay in the back room." As if suddenly he remembered, and said, "Yes, straighten up the back room, change the bed linen and all that." Rose assured him that she would.

Rose was mopping the veranda when a tall, lanky, young man with freshly-cut black hair came to the gate. Rose identified him right away. Nico had refused to go and get him at the correctional centre. "Hey, Nico here?" Rose told him Nico wasn't there.

"I'm his nephew Tony, he should be expecting me. Do you know when he's coming back?" His eyes narrowed and his brows knitted.

"I'm not sure," Rose said, walking to the gate. "But you're right, he is expecting you. Come in." Rose opened the gate and let Tony in. "I am Rose. I work for Mr. Nico. Follow me." Rose took Tony to the back room. "This is your room," she told him. Tony had a little knapsack with him that he put over the doorknob and hung his jacket over the door. "You can put your things in the closet or the chest of drawers," she told Tony, pointing to the furniture. "You want something to eat?"

"Can I have a sandwich?" he asked. "Do you have bologna?" Rose told him she did. "And a root beer, if you have that." Nico had shopped for the things he thought Tony would like.

Rose saw that Tony's hands could use washing. "The bathroom is on the other side of the hall," she told him.

Rose brought Tony's food to the table and called him.

"Oh thanks. What'd you say your name was again?"

"Rose, Rose Tomlinson."

"Thanks Rose," Tony said and took the food back to his room.

As soon as Tony went to his room, Rose noticed cigarette smoke emitting from under the door of his room. "Oh boy," she mumbled and shook her head. "From the frying pan to the fire."

When he left his room to go to the bathroom, he bumped into Rose in the hallway. "Hey Rose," he said. His casualness toward her, annoyed her. "Where are you from, Jamaica?"

Rose told him yes and he told her that he could tell because her accent sounded like the Jamaican guys he had met at the center.

"Some of the best weed comes from Jamaica, man." He laughed as he said this. His compliment for Jamaican weed didn't endear him to Rose. Rose, stuck in her ways, and with Tony talking about weed, made her judge him as no good.

Tony stayed in his room, mostly talking on the telephone. He only came out for the kitchen and bathroom. This routine only lasted a couple of days. By mid-week, Tony began leaving the house right after Nico left in the mornings. He returned in under half hour and locked himself again in his room. The difference then was not the cigarette smoke streaming from his room, but the potent, yet familiar smell of marijuana, otherwise called weed and ganja in Jamaica. Rose knew the smell all too well. She and Arthur had rented out a room in their family house to a tenant who had the same habit as Tony. The tenant waited until Arthur left for work, then he'd light up his weed at the back of the house. It bothered Rose that the children were exposed to the marijuana smoke and she reported the tenant to Arthur who had evicted him immediately. So, Rose had first-hand experience of the smell of weed. She was surprised however, that smoking weed seemed as prevalent amongst the youths in Canada as in Jamaica.

Rose had no patience nor tolerance for smoke that triggered a cough and tightness in her chest. She tolerated Nico's cigarette smoking because he was her boss and her only choice was to walk off the job, and she wasn't ready to do that yet. *The sacrifices we make*, she often mumbled. The weed that Tony smoked became too much to take, and she felt she had to let Nico know what was going on behind his back. She studied Tony's ways. He knew that when Nico left home in the mornings, he returned home by 3 p.m. Tony left the house behind Nico, and returned after an hour or so of leaving. Of late, instead of Tony leaving the house, a young man, around his age, light brown hair, carrying a knapsack, visited him. He would sit on the veranda until the man arrived. He met him at the gate and he followed him to his room where the weed smoking began. The man wouldn't stay long. Rose surmised that the man with the knapsack must be Tony's dealer.

Rose wanted to tell Nico about what went on behind his back, during the daytime. She knew it would cause problems for him and his nephew and even his sister, and thought about the consequences all around. She prayed that Nico would find out on his own. *But how?* she'd ask herself. Well, Rose got lucky, because what was very transparent to Nico was that Tony was home all day eating and being lazy. He was cognizant of his grocery bill growing just as high as Tony's sandwiches, and he began to get on Tony's case to get out of the house and find a job. This was music to Rose's ears, and her lungs. Nico made certain that Tony left home the same time he did every morning to go and look for work. This went on for a month. Tony left the house every morning and came home at 4 p.m.; his eating habits never changed, it just shifted to the hours after he came home. Rose wondered if Tony was walking the streets all day and came home famished. Nico's grocery bill was still growing. He confronted Tony in the kitchen. "Hey buddy, what's going on here? You've been going out to work for weeks now, where's the pay you're getting?" Tony had no response. "Listen man, you've got to start making some contributions around here." Tony grumbled that due to his "juvie" record, he wasn't being hired. "So, what do you do in the day time?"

"I look for work, Uncle Nic. I'm just not getting any call-backs."

"Okay, I tell you what, I'll talk to the Gallo brothers, see if they could use another bricklayer or something at the site. As a matter of fact, I'll take you down there myself tomorrow."

Tony shrugged and said, "Whatever", as he carried his plate of food in one hand and his soda in the other, back to his room.

True to his word, Nico took Tony down to the construction site and got Tony a job.

Nico was happy, so was Rose; Tony wouldn't be around to smoke and trigger her asthma. Because what Rose knew, Nico didn't. She knew that Tony didn't really want to work, he would rather be at home smoking marijuana, clogging up her lungs, and eating his sky-high bologna sandwiches with cans of root beer.

One day around noon, Tony came home looking beaten. He stepped past Rose and went straight to his room. Rose thought it odd, for Tony was consistently going out to work at the job site every morning, for weeks, coming home at six o'clock or later. Nico came home that same evening, fuming, and he too went past Rose and went straight to Tony's room. Rose hurried behind Nico. Nico went to Tony's room and flung the door open, "Hey mister!" Spit flew from Nico's mouth, his eyes bulged and he shouted, "Are you a goddamn imbecile? You damn idiot! How could you go smoking marijuana on the job?" Rose worried for Nico's health: he didn't need an induced heart attack.

Tony leaped from the bed. "Unc, uncle, I can explain."

"What can you explain? How you just lost the only job you could get?"

"Uncle Nic, let me explain." Tony looked as if he were about to cry. He had no real explanation and Nico was not going to have any excuses from him.

"I want you out of here! Now."

"But Uncle Nic, where am I going to go?" Tony said. Rose in the hallway taking it all in, wondered why Tony never thought of this before he started lighting up marijuana on the job.

"What do I care, damn it! I just want you out of here!" Nico said.

Rose observed the dynamic between Nico and Tony. As Nico took a turn to leave Tony's room, she pretended to be going to the bathroom and slipped inside, until Nico was in the living room.

"Please Uncle Nic, I know I goofed up, but please, please just give me one more chance." Tony walked in a circle around his uncle, apologizing.

"And I'm calling your mother. Let her deal with you." Nico called his sister and told her everything that transpired with Tony since he came to live with him. At the end of the call, Nico said, "Sure, sure thing, I agree with you." When Nico got off the call, he said to Tony, "Your mother wants you out there with her. I'll get you a ticket and you can leave tomorrow." Tony continued to plead that he wanted to stay there, in Toronto. "No. It's either Calgary, or on the streets of Toronto, I don't care. You can do what you want, but you're not staying in my goddamn house!"

Rose felt empathy for Tony, regardless of how she felt about his smoking in the house. She knew that he would be okay one way or the other. He was a young, white male, citizen of Canada and did not have to walk and look behind him anticipating immigration nor deportation. If he got into trouble, he had his family to assist him. Now her lungs could get some relief.

Rose stayed with Nico for a few more months. She continued to put up with him, as long as he didn't "pass his place" and let his hand "accidentally" touch her bottom. She deafened her ears to his slack and inappropriate comments with one aim in mind: to make enough money to provide what her children needed. Rose had no plans to solicit Nico to marry her for her landed status, so after one year of working with him, she sought employment elsewhere.

CHAPTER Twelve

Rose and Cynthia left home at eight o'clock in the morning, they headed to the suburbs of Toronto. Cynthia was taking Rose to her second job as an undocumented worker in Canada, a job she had secured for Rose with a long-time client of her husband. Rose remained quiet on the drive, looking out the window into her future, wondering how this new job would fare, compared to her last. It had been one year since she took the stance of not returning to Jamaica without landed status. Although being in Canada allowed her to take care of her family, she missed being with her children as they grew up. "Don't forget this is just another means to an end, one more employer means closer to getting your papers," Cynthia said, interrupting Rose's thoughts. "And if this don't work out, there's plenty more people wanting housekeeper, or day worker." Cynthia sped up, merging northbound unto the Don Valley Parkway. "Anyway, this is a whole household, much different from your last one employer, but you're there to do your work, and that's all anybody can ask for." Exiting the highway, Rose asked Cynthia to turn off the air conditioning, and she wound down the window. Rose caught sight of a family of five riding on the sidewalk. The father cycled in front, the three boys cycled behind him, and the mother rounded out the end. She smiled, seeing the family looking happy together. Her children had ridden tricycles as youngsters too. Donovan had asked for a bicycle for his last birthday that she hadn't bought, being too scared for him on the road. Her smile spread to her eyes, and she was pleased that she hadn't given him that gift. She didn't have to worry about getting a call about an accident. She bit her lips to stifle her emotions.

"You hear what me saying Rose?"

Rose heard Cynthia, even though her mind was locked on her children. She had become an illegal in Canada for one reason: to make money she wouldn't make in Jamaica. She was at the point where she did not need persuading to be a domestic helper, although illegal, in Canada. She would make this job work if it took braving the winter elements, and living a life dodging immigration. She needed to grow a thick skin. A recent call from her mother informed her that the landlord had raised the rent, again. Rose telephoned the landlord herself and told him, "Me have to wait on the bus in the freezing cold, morning and evening to go to work like a slave, take all kinds of garbage from people just to get a pay cheque. Listen to me carefully, you not getting any increase 'til you blasted well fix up the house." Yes, labouring in the cold in Canada had given Rose a thicker skin. Her mother told her that the landlord was there with the plumber the following day.

Cynthia reached the stoplight at Eglington and Don Mills and raised her head in the north-east direction, she said, "That's where Mr. George Bernhard works." She glanced at Rose. "Your new boss, him work in that building." Rose craned her neck to see behind Cynthia, the IBM building on the corner. "He's some manager over there." Cynthia was proud of her connections. She had kept in touch with the people from her husband's company, and a few of his customers. George's father had been one of Irv's long-time customers; Irv had done the books for his tailoring business. Later, Irv had become George's accountant.

Making a left turn onto Don Mills, Cynthia said, "He and his wife, Victoria, are good people, you'll like them. If you play your cards right, they might sponsor you." Rose nodded pensively. "And before you know it, you'll have your papers and can send for your children." Sounded good to Rose. The steering rolled through Cynthia's hands as she told Rose, "We're not far now." Rose sat up straight, focusing on the route and the bus number. "You have the phone number in case of anything?" Cynthia asked.

Rose opened her black handbag. "I have it memorize, but I still write it down," she said, fishing through the bag for the little piece of paper with Cynthia's telephone number. While in the bag, she opened her change purse to check for the last ten dollars she had folded and tucked away. Satisfied that she had the necessities, Rose fixed the bag on her shoulder and ignored the knot in her stomach. Cynthia turned onto the avenue. She drove to a white bungalow and parked in the driveway facing a double-car garage. A dark-haired woman holding a toddler, opened the door. "That's Victoria Bernhard," Cynthia said, before they exited the car.

Rose relaxed a little as the woman approached them smiling. "Come in, ladies," she said, and closed the door behind them.

"Thanks, ma'am," Cynthia said, and she and Rose tiptoed around the toys scattered on the floor. "Mrs. Bernhard, this is Rose, the lady I told you about." Rose noticed Cynthia's twang, and her demeanour, one of a prim and proper uptown Jamaican. *But that was Cynthia.* Rose smiled to herself. *She will be what she must be for any occasion.*

Rose and Mrs. Bernhard shook hands as they said hello and Rose liked the friendliness in Mrs. Bernard's manner. "Ms. Vickie is fine," she told Rose. "And this is little Tommy." Mrs. Bernard offered Rose and Cynthia a seat, and explained that her husband was at work, and their two girls were at school.

The ladies sat on the sofa by the window and Mrs. Bertrand pulled up a chair to face them with the boy in her lap. Rose brushed to the side a toy truck, and a couple of toy soldiers next to her on the seat. The baby saw Rose moving his toys and fussed to leave his mother's lap, pointing at Rose. Mrs. Bernhard smiled as she put him on the carpeted floor, and he waddled over to Rose.

"You're a big guy, Mr. Tommy," Rose said and enquired, "How old him is?" His mother confirmed that Tommy was just a big boy that looked much more than his eighteen months.

"He is going to be big like his father, we can already tell," Cynthia said.

The dark-haired boy dropped himself onto Rose, grabbing at the toy she playfully held behind her. He climbed onto the chair between Rose and Cynthia and did not fuss when Rose drew him closer and gave him the little toy soldier. He quickly grabbed it out of her hand, and held it to the side, wanting her to come after it the way he did.

Mrs. Bernhard laughed and clapped, her hands striking together like tambourines in a pocomania church sister's hand. "Rose, Tommy loves you," she said. Rose playfully bobbed the plumped-cheek boy on her knees, his almost full set of teeth nibbled on the rubber soldier in his hands. Mrs. Bernard commented that the boy and Rose bonding so early was a good sign, and that she was ready to go back to work after injuring her back and taking off an extra month. She thanked Cynthia, who knew she was on maternity leave and called at the right time, suggesting Rose as a nanny. "Rose, can you start work next week?"

The women looked at each other, their eyes aglow. These were words they both had hoped to hear. It had been a few weeks between jobs for Rose, and she had become accustomed to having a steady income to support her family back home.

Cynthia saw that Rose's demeanour was her old self, worried, so Cynthia was not at ease and made some connections. A sprawling smile covered Cynthia's face and her "yes", drowned out Rose's "yes".

"Sure, she would be more than happy to", and nudging Rose, said, "For as I told you, Rose has four lovely children of her own." She turned to Rose. "Rose, tell her about the children."

Rose was understandably reserved; this would be her first live-in job. She wanted to pinch herself, but Cynthia's poking made it real and quelled some of the nervousness. Her recent and only job was with one employer, Nico. Caring for her three girls and a boy was her only certification for working with children.

"My children are not babies anymore," she told Mrs. Bernhard. "Them all have them own interest that don't allow me so much to have my hands on them anymore, just my mind and my heart." Rose sighed lightly.

Mrs. Bernhard said, "I wish mine were teens, they'd be out of the hard-to-hear stage and give a little less talking." Rose asked their ages. "Sophie is ten and Mimi is eight." Mrs. Bernhard smiled proudly. "But they are good girls."

Although Rose was unfamiliar with how Canadians raised their children, she knew one thing, and said, "All children respond to love and kindness." Mrs. Bernhard's face lit up cherry-red, and when Rose added, "Yet a little discipline won't hurt just the same, it's a good teacher, I know." Mrs. Bernhard nodded in agreement.

Michelle Thompson

Tommy climbed into Rose's lap and rested his head on her chest. Cynthia said, "Wow, looks like he wants her to start today." All three women laughed, bonding over a promising future.

"This makes me happy, really happy," Mrs. Bernhard said and went straight into explaining the working conditions. "Rose," she said, sitting at the edge of her seat, her face looking pleased. "If you'll have us, the work is Monday to Friday, and Saturday until midday. You'll have Saturday afternoon and Sundays off." Rose's eyes widened, what she heard sounded reasonable. Mrs. Bernhard continued to explain that she and her husband left for work around 7 a.m. and arrived home between 6 – 6:30 p.m. and that Sophie and Mimi met their school bus at 7:45 a.m., which brought them back around 3:15 p.m. She led her to the window and showed her how near the bus was parked.

As Mrs. Bernhard laid out their routine, Rose pictured herself into the job, finishing her chores by the time the girls' school bus dropped them off. Cynthia, also listening to Mrs. Bernhard state the job requirements, and the $400 pay per month, was just as excited for her friend's prospects, and quickly answered, "Yes, ma'am, that would suit her fine." Rose, not sure if it was a reasonable amount that was offered, was thankful when Cynthia answered, and glanced at Cynthia with eyes that said, *we'll discuss it later.*

Tommy sat on Rose's lap, nibbling on the head of his little toy soldier, his mouth water dripped on her hand and lap. She dabbed his suckling mouth with the bib around his neck. When his mother offered a tour of the three-bedroom house, Rose carried him from room to room, his head resting on her shoulder, his heart beating on her chest. The closeness gave Rose a positive feeling, and a quiet fluttering of the heart, brought her nanny position to life. She welcomed the start date, for keeping busy meant keeping fretful monsters at bay, and a sure roof over her family's head. Tommy fell asleep; Rose followed his mother to his room and placed him in his crib, setting the monitor on his bed as Mrs. Bernhard instructed. From his room they went on to the kitchen across the hall where she explained their taste and style of cooking. Baking a chicken, she said they only sprinkled "a pinch of salt" before putting it in the oven. As she wondered how a chicken without black pepper, paprika, onion, garlic and scotch bonnet would taste, Mrs. Bernard opened the fridge and showed her the fresh spices she used to season her food. They finished the tour in the basement. Downstairs was Rose's quarters, and a small room in the corner that doubled as the laundry and storage. "Rose, this is your room," the mistress said, and waved Rose in. Both Mrs. Bernhard and Cynthia waited at the door watching Rose as she took in her new living arrangements.

Rose's room was a quaint, wall-papered room. Her eyes roamed from the floral walls to the matching curtains, to the comforter on the double bed, to the beige shag carpet under her feet. When she spun around, there was another door she opened to the ensuite bathroom. She peeped into the laundry room where two baskets with loads of clothes laid waiting to be laundered. "Lots to remember, Rose, but I'm here, so just ask," Mrs. Bernhard said from the doorway, and led Rose back upstairs to the living room. Rose glanced at Cynthia as she got to the landing, out of Mrs. Bernhard's purview, and the two friends gave each other quick nods and agreeable smiles.

Rose left her new employer with optimism, similar to Cynthia saying that she felt a bond already. She could not wait to call her family to tell them she would begin working with the family the following week. By 6:30 p.m. assured that they all were home, she was on the telephone making that call to them. "I got the job." She explained that it was a family of five that she would be working with, mainly taking care of the children and that "things look promising". She told them she was not sure how often she would be allowed to call them, but that the employers appeared understanding of her having children of her own back home. Maybe with her day off on Sundays, she could go to Cynthia and call from there. With their telephone on speaker, the children all chimed in to tell her that they missed her, and that she was doing the right thing and they understood why she had to stay in Canada. Rose was happy that they were understanding, but it still didn't ease the pain of her guilt and missing them so much.

Maureen hastened to give her mother news of their father, which garnered from Rose a kiss-teeth, and "I don't care if him know I'm in Canada, just don't give him the address, please!"

To which the children concertedly pleaded a resounding, "No Mommy!"

Mari took the phone next. Rose was filled with emotion as she encouraged her to keep up with her doctor's appointments, not to rely too much on the garlic tea and to always use the money she was sending to buy her blood pressure medication.

"But sometimes the children need something right away, Rose, and I have to get it for them. Don't forget the school fee for them is very high."

"Momma, listen to me now, I want you to have the medication over everything else. I don't want you to substitute your medicine with any bush tea. Because, if they don't have you, there is no school to go to, because you all agree that I should stay and work, so I need you to be alive and well out there." Her mother counselled her not to worry, that they would work it out. She warned Rose that it was more prudent that she kept good health for the cold season ahead, and to focus on doing what was necessary to get the family up there with her, soon. She ended the call by reminding Rose that she was praying for her. Her mother's words strengthened her and gave her hope for the future.

Mrs. Bernhard asked Rose to make an exception and start work on the upcoming weekend, to give her the weekend to prepare for work on Monday. This was fine with Rose, and on Saturday morning, Cynthia drove her to her new job. Mr. and Mrs. Bernhard came to the door to meet her. Smiling nervously, Rose stuttered her greetings to Mr. Bernhard; he comforted her by telling her to feel at home. He took the light jacket she wore and hung it in the closet by the entrance, and her small suitcase, he took to her room in the basement. He led her back upstairs to his office adjoining the living room. He stretched his hand to a chair next to his desk, inviting her to sit, and her nervousness eased.

"If you could put Tommy to sleep in fifteen minutes of meeting him, we're off to a great start."

Rose smiled, warming to her employer. "Thanks Mr. Bernard," she said. Her employer told her to call him George. Her Jamaican etiquette wouldn't allow her to call her employer by his first name, so she answered, "Yes, Mr. George." Just then the girls ran into the room, Tommy behind them. They showed off their pink tutus with specific attention to the frill around their waist. He introduced them. "This is Sophie, really Sophia, ten years old." Her brown hair up in a bun, she wasn't shy and spun around taking a bow for her father and Rose. "Come here sweetie, come say hello to Rose," he called the smaller one, dodging behind her sister. She ran into his arms and hugged his neck, clearly daddy's little girl. She stared at Rose when her daddy said, "And this is Mimi." He removed her balled-up fingers from her mouth. "A little shy, she's going on eight."

Rose told them that they looked like princesses and the girls giggled. Tommy came and leaned on Rose's lap. She picked him up, and in picking him up, remembered that the boy was weighty. She held him in her lap. "You remember me?" she asked, bouncing him on her knees. "Do you remember me?" She tickled his tummy. Tommy pursed his lips into a shy smile and wiggled, bending backwards out of Rose's hands. She stood him up on the carpeted floor and he ran back to his sisters' room. George was a stocky man, Rose saw where Tommy got his budding physique and thick, wavy black hair.

"He really likes you, Rose," said George pleasantly, as he watched the interaction with his son and new nanny.

Mrs. Bernhard and the girls stopped to get their jackets from the front closet, and said goodbye from the door. Tommy lingered at the door, fussing to go with them. Rose went after him as Mrs. Bernhard asked, and the boy pulled from Rose and clung to his mother's leg. Her kisses and promise of treats on her return, quieted him.

Rose let him stand with her at the doorway, until his sisters boarded the back of the grey, Honda mini-van. His sisters threw him kisses as their mother drove off and soon they were out of sight.

"Let's talk about your pay," Mr. Bernhard said. Rose drew her chair closer and put Tommy to sit at her feet with his little soldiers in each hand. "Not sure if my wife went over everything, but—" Rose told him that she gave her an idea and said that he would discuss the details. "It's a hundred and twenty-five dollars per week." Her eyes casted up, she tried a quick calculation of the Canadian currency into Jamaican dollars and realized she hadn't kept up to date to know the rate of exchange. "You will get a cheque weekly or bi-weekly, your preference?"

"Bi-monthly, sir," she blurted, surprised she had a choice. The pay was a little less than her previous job, but the home environment was better. Mr. Bernhard agreed to pay Rose $125.00 cash every other Friday. This worked for her plans to begin sending money back home every two weeks, instead of monthly. The amount of pay, although a little less than her prior job, was welcomed. After her last job, she had not worked for a few weeks, and was down to her last $20. She fought back a chuckle, brought on by a memory of her interaction at the Canadian airport. To her relief, the day she had flown into Canada, the immigration officer hadn't questioned the twenty dollars she had declared for her three-week stay in Canada; but it was the unfavourable stories she had heard of regarding other people and the limited amount, or no money that they were bringing into the country, which impeded their landing. She had walked away from the officer, not believing her luck. In planning her travels to Canada, knowing she may not return to Jamaica, her main concern was leaving the most money for her family.

Tommy dozed off on the carpet with his toy soldier partially in his mouth. Rose quickly took it from him and carried him to his room. She placed him in his crib, put on the monitor, and went to the kitchen. A few dishes were in the sink and while washing them, she wondered what to prepare for lunch. Mr. Bernhard, dressed in a navy-blue track suit, and a towel around his neck, came into the kitchen. He saw Rose doing the dishes by hand, and said, "Rose, you don't need to do that, we have a dishwasher."

He sounds just like Cynthia, Rose thought. She told him that she did not mind because washing by hands came naturally. She said, "I have been doing this nearly all my life. I like to feel the warm, soapy water on my hands." She looked at her hands after saying this and saw how wrinkled they had become, and right then thought to reconsider using the dishwasher.

"Okay, if you say so. Anyway, I'm running to the gym, Vickie and the girls should be back by noon." Rose asked him about lunch. "Mac and cheese is good, or mashed potatoes, and there is chicken in the fridge if you get hungry."

He took his water bottle from the fridge and put it and the towel in his gym bag. On his way out the kitchen he said, "Vickie will bring home groceries, and decide on dinner."

Rose was alone in the home after Mr. Bernhard left. Her quiet nervousness started dissipating and finally the calm and mental clarity she longed for, came. Being alone without anyone's input, not even her friend Cynthia, she could carefully decipher her next move. She quickly finished tidying the kitchen and dashed to the basement. She stood at the door of her room, slowly taking it in. A picture of the family lounging at the beach, Vickie holding baby Tommy and the girls nestled beside their daddy, hung on the wall. The picture reminded her of her own family in better days, when Arthur had taken their family to the Gunboat Beach in Kingston and had taught the children how to swim.

She sighed, and drew her suitcase closer. Between the vanity and chest of draws, she had more than enough space for her belongings. She sat on the bed to unpack. As she put her clothes in the vanity drawers, she caught a glimpse of herself in the mirror. She examined her face, turned her head from side to side, and told herself she had lost weight. Her eyes trailed down the rest of her body and convinced her that she was not looking the same in the year she had been to Canada. She had been putting off treating herself, only focusing on sending nearly every cent she earned in a money order or a barrel to home. Rose decided that she should get her hair done, and with her current size, buy some new clothes.

From what Ms. Vickie had told Rose, she guessed that Tommy would be asleep for a few hours. This allowed her to sort her clothes, while keeping track of the time to start the laundry, and go upstairs to the kitchen. Separating the Mrs. from the Mr.'s clothes, Rose was shocked by what she came upon: a couple of menses-soiled panties wrapped in a towel. She squirmed when she saw it. Rose dropped the towel with the panties in the bucket at the side to soak, for separate washing. "Lord Jesus Christ," she said out loud, "is this what me going to have to deal with, every blastid month?" Rose didn't know what to do, she wanted to throw them out, but thought that Ms. Vickie might miss them. Tears came to Rose's eyes. She felt less than, helpless and pitiful in that moment for not having an alternative to working with Ms. Vickie. She had never had to handle soiled underwear for anyone other than herself and her daughters. Not even for her last employer, Nico, who didn't wear underpants. Rose sat silently for a moment. She pondered, oh what a day, when she'd be free of domestic work and all the trauma it brought. She forced back tears and carried on, because in the end, she had no choice.

She learned to multi-task around the house quickly, sticking to the schedule she and Cynthia had made. As the washing machine churned, she cleaned the bathrooms and vacuumed the three bedrooms. She prepared the girls' lunch before tackling the living room filled with all kinds of toys and books. She put the toy cars in the bin, set Barbie and Ken side by side on the sofa, and stacked the books by size against the wall. Although she had turned on the monitor in Tommy's room, she checked on him before starting the vacuum, and closed his door behind her. The telephone rang a few times, but she did not answer it, as she was not instructed to do so. The last time it rang, it woke Tommy and he got up crying. Rose hurried with his bottle to him, and he continued to lay down and feed himself. She had just a small area in the living room to complete, which she did and then Tommy had her to himself.

It was two o'clock, two hours past the time of Ms. Vickie's expected return. As it was the first Saturday on this schedule, Rose did not know what to think. Would Ms. Vickie always be home at the time she said, or was this an exception and reason for concern? Ms. Vickie had left her phone number and other important numbers pasted on the phone. Rose thought of calling her but wondered if she would appear presumptuous to question her employer's whereabouts. She was hoping Mr. George would have been back by now, but alas. She chastised herself for not answering the phone when it rang in case it was Ms. Vickie calling to say she was delayed. Rose sat at the window with Tommy in her lap, or sometimes she'd paced the floor, looking out for the family to drive into the driveway.

Tommy wiggled himself to the floor to play with his toys, and in no time, he was laying on his tummy fast asleep. Rose picked him up and he awoke, crying. She tried him with his bottle, and he finished it and fell asleep in her lap. Rose took him to his room to freshen him up and change his clothes, and to put him back to sleep. In the middle of tidying Tommy, Rose heard the front door open and the girls running in. Tommy heard them too. He sprung up in the crib, not allowing Rose to finish dressing him. "Momma," he called, continuously twisting from Rose. She had to let him go, and he ran into the living room to meet his mother and sisters.

"Hey Rose, sorry I'm late," Ms. Vickie said. "I was calling to let you know we were going to be a little while coming home." Rose explained that she wasn't sure if she should answer the phone. "Even if George or I are home, you can get it." She gave Rose one of the grocery bags and she carried the other. Rose and the children trailed her to the kitchen. "The girls had a birthday party to attend after dancing that I forgot all about." She started unpacking the grocery bags. Rose went to the counter and helped her to pack the things in the fridge and cupboards, so she could pick up Tommy who was clamouring to get into her arms.

"Did you want me to fix supper Ms. Vickie?'

"No, me and the girls, we're alright for now." Her daughters sandwiched her with Tommy in her arms. "They stuffed themselves with so much cake and ice cream, and I had lasagna and pizza." Mimi and Sophia spoke over each other to tell Rose that they also had hot dog and chips. "So, we're full."

Rose was relieved that she didn't have to go back into the kitchen to cook close to eight o'clock in the night. "What about Mr. George, Ms. Vickie?"

"I brought home some lasagna; he can have that if he's hungry." Little Tommy spun from side to side in his mother's lap. "Is he hungry?" Ms. Vickie asked Rose.

"I feed him not too long ago. He might just want to sleep. He took a nap earlier today." Ms. Vickie put Tommy over her lap and rocked him. "Rose, could you draw a bath for the girls?" The two sisters walked tippytoe, the little ballerinas they were, behind Rose to the bathroom. Rose drew their bath and left the sisters in the tub to play in their bubble bath. She rejoined Ms. Vickie in the kitchen. "On Sunday mornings we like to sleep in. The girls like to get up and have breakfast then they go back to their room to watch television or whatever they like, which is mostly watching TV." Rose asked what they liked to have for breakfast. "They'll tell you," Ms. Vickie said. "Oh, and for dinner tomorrow, I bought a roast."

Mr. Bernhard came home shortly after his wife and daughters. He came through the door, threw his keys down on the entryway table, and shouted that he was home. Tommy stretched his hands to go to his father and soon as he went to his father, he ran back to his mother's arms. They started to discuss their day, and Rose excused herself. "I'm just running downstairs, if you need me."

"Check in on the girls for me, please," Ms. Vickie told Rose. "They should be ready to get out of the tub now before they dry up like raisins." She chuckled.

"Okay Ms. Vickie."

"We'll call if we need you." They left the living room for their bedroom, taking Tommy with them.

The girls were too busy playing with their dolls to realize that their bathwater had become flat and chilly, and although they were trembling from the draft, they never seemed to mind.

"Rose, come and look at this," Sophia said to Rose as she entered the bathroom. She showed Rose how her doll could swim under the water, then made her miraculously walk. Mimi, not to be out done, showed Rose how her doll could walk on the edge of the bathtub, and do backsplits. The two sisters certainly knew how to be each other's company.

"Nice, very nice. But your mother says it's time to come out of the tub." The girls protested that they weren't ready. "But look at how the two of you shaking, you must be cold." Of course, the girls said they weren't, through shivering lips. Rose wrapped their towels around them and lifted them out of the bathtub. "You can do it again tomorrow," she told the pouting sisters, insisting that they didn't want to wait until tomorrow, that they wanted to continue today. Rose knew their mother wouldn't let them, so she said, "I tell you what, I'll beg your mother for more bath time for you tomorrow, okay?"

Both girls yelled, "Yeah! Yeah! Yeah!" They skipped out of the bathroom to their bedroom.

Rose smiled at the three of them bonding; happy that she had discovered early, one thing it took to get on their good side.

"Rose," Mimi said, almost a whisper; Rose picked her up. Still wrapped in her towel, Mimi chewed on the end of it.

"Rose," she said again. Rose removed the towel from her mouth and told her to go ahead. "Can I ask you something?" Mimi said, shyly. "Can you take us to the park tomorrow?"

"Sure," Rose answered. She didn't know if Ms. Vickie had specific plans for them on Sunday, however, she did not think she would object to her taking them to the park. Rose assisted them to put on their pyjamas.

"We don't go to bed this early," Sophia told Rose. Rose pointed out that it was almost nine o'clock. "We don't put on our night clothes until we are going to sleep."

"Well, you just had a bath, you're smelling so nice and fresh, you might as well put on your clean nighty, so if you fall asleep, you're already in your night clothes, right?" She tickled Sophia's tummy and Mimi drew closer for her tickle.

Sophia started to jump on her bed and Mimi joined her to see how high each could out-jump the other. Sophia jumped so high she almost fell off the bed. Rose warned them a couple of times to be careful. "I won't fall, I'm superwoman, can't you tell?" Sophia said and giggled.

"Just be careful alright,"

"What would you do if I fell on the floor and burst my head?" Sophia asked, teasingly.

"I don't think your parents would like that."

"Yeah, but I want to know what you'd do?" Rose wasn't sure what Sophia was getting at and asked her why she asked. "I just wanna know. Would you spank me?"

"Do you want me to spank you?" Sophia stopped jumping; she calmed down and shook her head, no.

She sat beside Rose at the edge of the bed. "Do you have any children Rose?" When Rose told her she did, she wanted to know how many, and Rose told her four. "Are they big or are they small?" Rose told her their ages. "And do you spank them?"

"Yes, I spanked them." Rose realized Sophia was testing the boundaries with her. "Yes, I spanked them when they do rude things, but I wouldn't spank you."

"Why, why wouldn't you spank me Rose, because I'm little?"

"No, because you and your sister are not my children."

"My last babysitter spanked me and my dad got rid of her," Sophia said and pouted. "I'm glad she's gone!"

"Well, I don't believe it is my place to spank you. I should be able to discipline you, you know, tell you right from wrong, but not hit you."

"Yeah! Yeah Rose! I like you." Sophia raised her hands in victory, then hugged Rose's neck, and Rose felt a sincere warmth from her. Sophia then ran her hand up and down Rose's arm, observing her skin: the colour, the texture, the protruding veins, looked at hers in comparison, and said, "You have a different colour than me." She stared at Rose's face. "You are black." Rose acknowledged that Sophia was correct.

"But see", Rose put her hand against theirs, "See, we have different colour, but we are the same. I have eyes, mouth, and nose just like you girls."

Mimi rubbed Rose's hand. "Is your hand dirty?"

Sophia swiftly elbowed her younger sister, and said, "No, it's not dirt. She is black. Don't you understand, she has black skin."

"But how come?" Mimi looked puzzled. "Because you're from Jamaica?" she asked.

In a different circumstance, Rose could have been offended and want to defend herself from someone asking if she was dirty. Nevertheless, Rose saw the innocence, a genuine wanting to know this information, from a child. She smiled, thinking of how to answer in a manner that a ten and eight-year-old could understand. "Do you know about God?" Rose looked from one girl to the other. "Do your parents tell you about God?" Rose held her breath, hoping that God wouldn't be a stranger to the girls. She remembered seeing a picture of Jesus and his disciples hanging on the wall in the sitting room.

Sophia shook her head to say yes, as her little sister yelled, "God lives up in the sky in heaven."

"No, he doesn't." Sophia gave Mimi an annoying glance. "He doesn't live up in the sky." Sophia, irritated by her younger sister's youthful ignorance, clarified for her. "He lives everywhere", she made a circle with her hands that followed with "And inside of us", pointing to her chest "Me", and touching her sister's, "You."

"We pray to Jesus and God all the time," Mimi said, happily.

Her sister agreed, adding, "Every night."

"That means you know that God made all of us, right?" The girls leaned on Rose, listening eagerly, and nodded that they knew. "Well God made all the people in the world, like here in Canada and Jamaica, all over the world. And he loves all the people just the same, no one is better than the other, only some have different skin colour."

"You mean like the people of Jamaica have black skin and the people of Canada have white skin?"

"Not really. You can come from Canada and have black or brown or white skin, same as in Jamaica."

The girls looked askance at Rose. Mimi's brows kitted, her eyes narrowed. "What?" she said, squinting. "I don't understand."

Sophia said, "I don't get it, Rose."

Rose recognized that she had lost the little ones, and some things had to wait until they were more mature in their thinking. "It is complicated."

"It's what?" Mimi said.

"Alright, alright," Rose said. "Let me try to explain."

Rose told the girls that God could do anything, and he could make different people live in different places. "Because he is

God, and he can do all things." She stretched her hands wide open to emphasized "all". The girls shook their heads slowly, thoughtfully. "And that is why God says that we must love each other, no matter what's the colour of our skin." The girls remained quiet, snuggled up to Rose, taking it in. Rose wanted to make sure her points got across, and said, "Get it?" The girls nodded. "Okay then." Rose clapped. "It's time for bed." Mimi ran over to her bed and climbed on, and Sophia pulled her pillow under her head. Rose pulled the cover sheet up to the girls' chests and turned off the ceiling light for the nightlight. "Good night little ones, see you in the morning."

The girls answered in unison, "Good night, Rose."

"Is that you, Rose?" Ms. Vickie said, as Rose walked by her bedroom. Rose put her head through the opened door to acknowledge Ms. Vickie. "Could you put Tommy in his crib?" Ms. Vickie asked. "I won't let him sleep with me anymore, he has to get used to sleeping in his own bed at nights."

Rose put the boy in his crib, set the monitor and went downstairs to her quarters. Heading to the bathroom, she passed the laundry room and glimpsed the mountain of clothes she had washed that was waiting to be ironed. Tomorrow, she told herself. Right then, she remembered she had told the girls that she would take them to the park, and suddenly, she wasn't so sure that she could. Still, she had promised them in their bonding and wanted to keep her word. She would have to rearrange her work schedule to make going to the park happen.

It was a long day for Rose, her first day working with the family of five. In bed that night, she reflected on the day, her chores and responsibilities. She was hired primarily for little Tommy but realized that the job comprised of being responsible for the entire household, and the chores that came along with the house. This, she would speak with Cynthia about, she noted.

A Way To Escape 2

By the end of the first week, Rose was looking forward to beginning her weekend time off. Saturday morning, Ms. Vickie took the girls to their dance class, and Mr. George went to the gym with the understanding that they would be back early afternoon for Rose to leave. While they were gone, Rose busied herself with her chores, looking forward to their return so she could be on her way to Cynthia's. Around 1:30 p.m., what a joy it was for Rose when Ms. Vickie pulled up in the driveway and Mr. George drove in behind her.

Rose's expectations ran high. Everything was on track and her plan so far was unfolding without a hitch. Rose met the family at the door with a big smile. All doubts were out the window: the house was spotless, little Tommy was asleep and lunch was simmering on the stove; she was rearing to go. She helped Ms. Vickie and Mr. George to take the groceries to the kitchen and packed them away. After Rose gave them a rundown of her morning, she said, "Can you let me know what else you'd like me to do? And then I'll call Cynthia so she can come and get me."

"Ah Rose," Ms. Vickie said, looking at her husband. Rose's heart skipped a quick beat; she held her breath. "We have, George and I, have an engagement this evening, and –" Ms. Vickie said tactfully.

Mr. Bernard chimed in, "Yes, Rose, Vickie and I have a function this evening and we'd like it if you could watch the kids while we were gone." Mr. George spoke more forthrightly than his wife, but with a "hey-buddy, just-asking-a-favour-grin".

Rose couldn't believe her ears. All those horrible stories of domestics getting shortchanged on their days off, or straight out denied it, flooded her mind. Rose kept a straight face without showing her disappointment. She was so much looking forward to spending some quiet time away from the children whom she had quickly grown attached to. At Cynthia's, she had planned to call her family, and just be in the company of her friends, Cynthia and Gurley.

Rose's expectation blew out like a punctured tire. Nonetheless, she continued in hope. Not having the courage to voice her disappointment about not getting her Saturday afternoon off, Rose gave the couple the benefit of the doubt that they'd be home early enough for her to begin her weekend. Despite being hopeful, Rose had a tinge of doubt. She wasn't sure a reception at 6 p.m. would give them enough time to enjoy themselves, and be home early enough to relieve her. She wrestled with these feelings, as she watched the clock for the couple's return. This was a conversation she wanted to have with Cynthia, yet she was scared to use the phone for fear her employers might call and found the telephone line busy. Rose, anxiously waiting, kept herself occupied by playing with the children. Soon the children got tired, so she gave them a snack, tidied them and put them to bed.

Rose herself went to bed at 9:30 although she did not sleep; she stayed awake listening for the husband and wife to come home. The clocked ticked away, and 9:30 became 10:30, then 11:30. Rose wasn't sure when she dozed off but jumped out of her sleep by the sudden laughter of Ms. Vickie and Mr. George, entering through the front door. She looked at the clock-radio that read 12:35 and sighed heavily. Plans to begin her weekend off was out of the question. No sitting and laughing with Cynthia and Gurley as they enjoyed their Sunday dinner. Gurley had received her Canadian resident status and Rose was looking forward to her relaying the joys of her dream come true and plans for her next steps. Rose wondered when her turn would come to free herself from domestic work, and unreliable employers. Rose felt her tears balling up, and she turned onto her side and cried herself to sleep.

Months passed and Rose got no weekends off. She had become accustomed to her employers' deceit around giving her time off. It was one reason or the other, one evening engagement after another or going away on the weekend and taking Rose with the family. Rose soon realized that she was not only a nanny for little Tommy when Ms. Vickie went to work, but she was the babysitter for all the children, and the caretaker of the entire family. She learned not to trust their ways, and for this reason, she did not approach them about assisting her with getting her landed documents.

Eight months after she started working with the Bernhards, George got a promotion in Seattle, U.S.A and the family moved away.

Rose was out of work again and moved back to Cynthia. Gurley had moved to her own place and Cynthia was glad to have Rose back, and already had a job lined up for her.

Chapter Thirteen

Rose began working for Mr. and Mrs. Pettiepiece two years into her stay in Canada, her third employment as an undocumented, "illegal" worker.

Shortly after coming to Canada on a visitor's visa to her friend Cynthia, Cynthia's next door neighbour Mr. Pettiepiece fell ill, and was rushed to the hospital. Cynthia surmised that when Mr. Pettiepiece came home from the hospital, he'd most likely need a caregiver to assist his elderly wife, a position that Rose could fill. Two years and two employers later, Rose was being considered for the job of his caregiver.

Rose received a call from Mrs. Pettiepiece inviting her for a visit. Mr. Pettiepiece had been recovering at home with only his wife's help, and the occasional assistance from their two children, daughter Margret and son Gordon, who lived in the U.S. and Australia respectively. When he was discharged from the hospital, both children came to Toronto to spend a month each helping their parents, although it was Margret who consistently took the trek to Toronto to help her mother with her father. Gordon, the older, had a family and business in Australia, and Margret unmarried, with less responsibilities, volunteered to take time off from her teaching job to assist them. Margret was currently visiting, and at the end of a four-month leave, it was time for her to return to work and her life in California.

Mrs. Pettipiece and Margret welcomed Rose into the home and all three sat in the living room to converse about Rose's potential as the Pettipieces' helper. Rose felt she had become seasoned to working in Toronto as a caregiver and this time, did not need to be escorted by Cynthia. She was ready for the interview, or so she thought. "Rose, my mother told me you're a friend of her next-door neighbour, Cynthia."

"Yes, I am. I actually met your mother a couple years ago when your father was in the hospital, so I know some of the background info. As a matter of fact, I was here the day he was taken to the hospital." Rose tried to show Margret that she wasn't just any helper, she actually had some history with her father.

"So, you know that he is not totally out of the woods."

Rose nodded and said, "A heart attack is not a easy thing."

"He is bedridden for the most part."

"Is he able to walk?"

"Not really, he depends on a walker and a wheelchair, and my mother's shoulders."

"And she's a frail elder herself." Rose glanced at Mrs. Pettipiece sitting beside her, looking helpless.

"That's right." Margret shifted to the edge of her seat. "Tell me Rose, have you ever looked after someone that's bedbound?"

"No, but I can imagine it would take a lot to manage somebody like that. But that wouldn't bother me, I use to –" Rose was about to mention that she not too long ago had taken care of a toddler who couldn't do anything for himself and depended on her to bathe him, turn him and change his diaper, when it occurred to her that a baby was much lighter and easier to maneuver for changing and dressing, than a hundred and sixty-pound senior with not much flexibility.

"Working with my father will be a 24-hour operation, you know, quite demanding. And my mother, as it is, can hardly manage herself," Margret interjected.

Rose stared at Margret, absorbing her every word. "I understand, I understand ma'am."

"What I'm saying is—"

"No, I get it Ms. Margret, it going to be tough."

"Yes. My mother might also need you to help her from time to time."

"Oh yes, that's what I'd be here for, to help her with Mr. P."

"Not only with my dad, Rose, what I'm saying is, she will have her own care needs." Rose remained silent, deciphering what Margret said. "Do you understand me, Rose?" She understood quite well and wondered if Margret was scaring her out of the job. "So, while my father needs physical assistance," Margret continued, "feeding him, washing him, and not only that, but help with the occasional accident he might have on the way to the toilette." Rose made a big gulp that she nearly choked on, *oh boy*. She imagined how she would manage two senior citizens by herself, should Ms. Pettipiece become too tired, or worse, physically ill. The thought kept Rose frozen in her seat.

"Not to worry Ms. Margret." She sprung to life. "I just finish working for a family of five. I can get you a reference from them if you want."

"That's fine, that's fine Rose, my mom likes you so that's half the battle won." Rose looked at Mrs. Pettipiece and smiled, and thank God she and her husband had stopped smoking. "Have you ever fell asleep while working?"

Rose wondered where that question had come from. "No ma'am, not me, I'm very careful," she confidently replied.

"What about administering medication, have you ever given the wrong meds or the wrong dose, or missed a dose altogether?"

"No ma'am." Rose knew that her not being a nurse, she was not allowed to do so. Cynthia had told her.

"I mean my mother will administer his meds, but you could watch to see it's going right. All his medication and schedule are pasted on their bedroom door."

Even though Rose tried to hide the sweat settling under her armpits, her sunken demeanour gave away a little doubt creeping in. "No ma'am, you can count on me. I'll do my best," she said, pulling herself together.

Margret let up a bit with her heavy questioning. "I hear you have four children in Jamaica?" Rose agreed she did. "You must miss them," Margret said with a softness in her voice.

Rose answered, "Yes, I do, very much", and remembered why it was necessary for her to withstand the torture of what felt like an interrogation.

"You know, me and my brother, we both live outside the country, so we'd want to be notified, called really, for anything pertaining to my father's health, and my mother for that matter. You know she's not that strong, and has recently been diagnosed with COPD herself." The thought of taking care of two sickly old people, suddenly wrecked Rose's nerves. Nervousness took hold and she hoped Margret couldn't tell. She and Cynthia had talked about if she played her cards right, Mrs. Pettipiece could sponsor her as Mr. Pettipiece's caregiver. Rose loved the sound of that and was not going to make Margret's questions intimidate her. She had too much at stake and was too close to getting her landed papers, and eligibility to get her children with her.

A bell rang in the back. "That's my dad," Margret said, getting up. Mrs. Pettipiece was already on her way down the hall with Margret in tow. Rose sat by herself for a little while, wondering what was happening; then she thought it wise to follow the women to check on Mr. Pettipiece. Rose stood at the door watching the mother and daughter care for Mr. Pettipiece. Margret eased between her mother and the bed and rolled her father unto his side. An act that normally took her mother more than twice as long with struggle, took Margret one fast swoop. Rose compared herself to Margret, a full-sized woman, almost two times her mother's petite size, and a couple of dress sizes bigger than Rose. Mrs. Pettipiece stepped aside and let her daughter shift her father to the edge of the bed and put him to sit up. She brought his walker to him and assisted him to hold onto it, guiding him from behind.

Rose moved into the room to get a close-up of Margret's movements. This would be the only training she'd receive regarding assisting a senior hands-on. Margret let her father walk to the bathroom with her assistance, but she toileted him once he got there. "I'm allowing my dad to help himself a bit. Because with me gone it's just going to be my mom alone with him, unless you can start right away, Rose." Margret had a sly grin, and although her smile was playful, she was very serious about Rose starting on the spot.

"I'm ready to start Ms. Margret, I have no other job right now."

Margret looked at her mother for confirmation. Mrs. Pettipiece answered, "Well, yes! That's why we called you over."

Rose told Mrs. Pettipiece, "Thank you ma'am." And to Margret, said, "Thank you Ms. Margret." Just those few minutes of watching Margret assist her father, gave Rose renewed confidence in her own capabilities to care for him.

"John, this is Rose," Mrs. Pettipiece told her husband, cheerily. She wanted him to feel excited that they both were getting permanent help. "That's Cynthia's friend, she lives with Cynthia, and guess what?" Mr. Pettipiece glanced at Rose then stared at his wife, waiting to hear the news. "Rose has agreed to come and help me take care of you." Mrs. Pettipiece spoke with such enthusiasm that Mr. Pettipiece looked back at Rose and nodded his approval with a smile. "What do you think, John?" Mr. Pettipiece nodded his agreement, his eyes focused on the steps he was taking back to bed.

"Yes, Dad, Rose will help mom as I'm leaving in a couple days. I've got to go back to work." Mrs. Pettipiece attempted to help Margret put her husband into bed.

Rose moved in, "Let me do it, Mrs. P.", and she and Margret held Mr. Pettipiece, each wrapped their hand around his back, and he hugged their necks, and on a count of three, they eased him up onto the bed.

"See Dad, you'll be in good hands with Rose and mom."

Mr. Pettipiece stared at Rose; his eyes searched hers. Rose said, "Yes, sir", equally holding his stare, "I will help you; you can count on me."

Margret put her father to bed and pulled the covers up to his neck the way he liked it. She kissed his forehead. "Ok, Daddy, continue to rest." Mrs. Pettipiece also reached over and kissed her husband and rubbed his hand. He smiled at his wife and daughter, and closed his eyes.

Mrs. Pettipiece and Margret walked Rose to the door. "I'm leaving Sunday evening, Rose, can you begin then?"

Rose was happy to be working with Cynthia so close. She planned how she would work at the Pettipieces' in the daytime, and go home, next door, in the evenings. This was until Mrs. Pettipiece quickly pointed out that nighttime was when she needed her the most, which was fine with Rose. Cynthia was only a chat at the fence away.

But things didn't remain fine for Rose. Four months into the job, she worked around the clock with no designated days off, and nights were just as demanding as days.

Mr. Pettipiece had medications to take at certain hours of the night and had to be awakened for them each time. Mrs. Pettipiece wanted to be hands-on with her husband's needs but didn't accept that she was unreliable in administering his nightly medications. Often, she slept through the alarm when it went off and it was Rose who woke and then woke her. Mrs. Pettipiece slept on a day bed by the window, across from her husband's bed. All Mr. Pettipiece had to do was shake his bell, and Mrs. Pettipiece would hear it from anywhere in the house. And since she slept in the same room as him, he only needed to call her. After getting up to care for her husband, she was unable to fall back to sleep. Her sleeping hours became erratic. She was falling asleep during the daytime, getting off schedule, and not able to assist Rose with her husband, as she had wanted. Rose realized that the time had come for Mrs. Pettipiece to get her own caregiver, but as long as Rose was there, she was expected to manage the care needs of two sick and frail seniors, including cooking, cleaning and laundry.

Rose reported this to Margret on one of her weekly telephone calls. Margret tried to "talk some sense" into her parents, but neither relented. Mrs. Pettipiece insisted that she must be involved in the needs of her husband. Margret, hundreds of miles away felt she had to give in. "In a way, I understand them," she told Rose. "My parents have been married for going on sixty years. They met in college. They don't know anyone else but each other." So, with things the way they were, Rose was basically on her own.

By six months of working under these conditions, one day at the fence, Rose opened up to Cynthia. "Boy, Cynthia, if you think Mrs. P. sleep deprive, it's me who long for a good night's rest. Sometimes, I feel like I going to drop down."

"I don't believe this is good for you Rose," Cynthia complained. "You one with the two of them? No man. And they both heavy care at this point." Rose shook her head. "Yes, Mrs. P. can do certain things for herself, yet she's not capable to be left alone to do anything concerning Mr. P." Rose simply listened as Cynthia stated the obvious and was glad she was in agreement. Cynthia stared in Rose's eyes to drive home this point. "You know you can't take the chance and fall asleep and leave the two of them, right? Because Mrs. P. will just fall asleep alongside you." The women chuckled. "And poor Mr. P., he will be there ringing the backside out of that bell, and no one to hear him. What a thing," Cynthia said. "Lord Jesus."

"I don't want to laugh, but if I don't laugh, I will cry," Rose said, and chuckled.

"Sometimes for your sanity, you have to laugh, yes," Cynthia reasoned.

"Cynthia, we can't take this thing for a laughing matter, you know that?"

"No, but it can be funny and serious at the same time. What you going do?"

Rose hissed. "Boy I really don't have any idea right now."

"You should tell the children what happening."

Rose said she told the daughter and she thought it was cute that her parents' love for each other was undying.

"Me tell you man, if me never start the work, if I had the slightest idea, me wouldn't have said yes to it." Rose took a deep breath and shook her head. "Because right now it stressing me out, bad, bad."

"I can just imagine, but you know, if you want good, your nose has to run," she said, reminding Rose of the old Jamaican colloquial that Rose knew too well. Her own mother reminded her a few times since she made the decision to stay illegally in Canada, that whatever good you wanted out of life, you had to be prepared to work hard for it.

"As a matter of fact, just last week, Mrs. P offer me more pay, say Margret said to give me fifteen dollars more per week."

"Fifteen dollars?" Cynthia raised her eyes up to the sky as if calculating. "Not great, but not that bad either."

"Yes, but no amount can make up for my health," she told Cynthia. "By the way, I don't even know where I would go for a doctor if something unfortunate happen to me."

"Missus, you worry too much."

"No man, this is a serious concern."

"Rose, don't me tell you already that you could go to my doctor, Dr. Baker, the same doctor Irv went to and now me?" Cynthia stared at Rose. "Stop your worrying man."

"And what if me have to go to hospital, me don't have no OHIP."

"Stop it Rose. What me say? You worry too much."

Rose hung her head.

"Easy for you to say, Cynthia, you not only landed, you're a citizen. Your bread butter two sides."

"I told you already, if anything should happen to you, the Canadian government wouldn't allow no hospital to bar you from getting treatment. This is not the U.S. Why you think people love Canada so much?"

"That's good to know," Rose said and sighed; a big weight came off her shoulders.

"I think it's a good time for you to talk to Mrs. P. about sponsoring you."

"You mean Margret?"

"No, me mean Mrs. P, or maybe the two of them together, because Mrs. P will be the actual one to do the sponsorship as Mr. P's. wife. She would apply under the basis that she needs you to help her with her husband." Rose listened intently. "And them better start applying now. Anything can happen to their health and they get worse, and the children put them in nursing home."

"Then me out of a job." Rose nodded at the realization.

"That's right. You out of a job and no money to send home."

"So, she can do it now, seeing that me not here three years yet?"

"Well, you almost have three years, and she can at least start, because it's not like she doesn't need the help now. And the application takes time."

Rose smiled, what Cynthia said, brought joy to her heart.

"Hold on little, let me go check on them." Rose went into the house and saw both Mr. and Mrs. Pettipiece were sound asleep.

She returned to Cynthia at the fence. "Hey Rose, guess who called yesterday?"

"Who? Roy?"

"Oh boy, you treat that man so bad. When you going make him happy and go out with him?" Rose looked at Cynthia anxiously. Cynthia continued, "You wouldn't believe."

Rose knitted her brow. "Who, who, Yvonne?"

"Yes, Yvonne. She have another baby, you know, a little girl this time."

"Wow. Nice. She must be so happy."

"Yeah man, she sounded overjoyed."

"I wonder if she got her papers yet?"

"Not yet, it's looking about she say, and she expect to send for her boy and her mother by next year."

"Wow, that's good. That's why we never hear from her, she was busy making baby." Rose and Cynthia laughed.

"Does she plan to come back here, even for a visit?"

"She never said. But she gave me her number to give you. She said she can't forget you." Rose teared up, her heart was glad again, she worried about the young waitress for months after she left without any contact. She breathed a sigh of relief, satisfied that she at last got some word about Yvonne. With a pleasing countenance, she said, "Me happy for her though. May God continue to bless her and her family."

Rose thought about what Cynthia said all night into the next morning, that starting her landed papers now made sense. She telephoned Cynthia in a quick call. "I am going to do it. I don't see why they wouldn't go along with helping me with my residency."

"You don't give them anything to worry about, and you working practically by yourself."

"Can you come over this evening and help me broach the topic with Mrs. P.?"

Cynthia made some mutton soup and brought some for Mrs. Pettipiece and Rose. Rose set the table for the three of them. "Thanks Cynthia," Mrs. Pettipiece said, as the women gathered around the table. "You know I love your soups."

They ate their meal amidst small talk and Rose encouraged them to move to the living room for tea and custard pie. The women flanked Mrs. Pettipiece on the sofa. Mrs. Pettipiece started bragging on Rose, how she had been a blessing to her and her husband. "I swear, Rose coming here has saved both mine and John's life."

"So, you owe me one, Mrs. P.," Cynthia said, jokingly.

"Oh, that's no joke, I tell you. I couldn't manage without her."

Rose's emotions stirred and she smiled broadly.

"So, you say she's a keeper?"

"You better believe she is." Mrs. Pettipiece looked from Cynthia to Rose. "And John has grown attached to her."

"Really?" Rose's smile lit up her eyes. "Thank you, ma'am."

"You're darn right, I am. Me and Margret were talking only yesterday when you were doing the laundry. And she said how you must miss your kids."

"Very much, ma'am, very much."

"She suggested that I talked to you about applying to immigration for your permanency."

"What, you mean sponsor me?" Words Rose wanted to hear but were also shocked by. *Mrs. P. must have read my mind.* She smiled with all her teeth on display.

"Yeah, why not? As a matter of fact, I've been meaning to speak with you about this Rose." Rose couldn't breathe, her heart was pounding. Her tears welled up and she glanced at Cynthia. Cynthia's face was lit up in a big, fat smile.

"Oh, that would be so nice, Mrs. P." Cynthia's eyes watered for her friend's good fortune. "When would you go to immigration to begin the filling, Mrs. P.?"

"Well, for Rose and I to leave the house, we'll need someone to stay with John."

"Oh Mrs. P. you wouldn't have to worry about that. I'm free tomorrow, and I say strike the iron while it's hot, can you go tomorrow?"

"Dr. Berger is coming to see me tomorrow afternoon but I'm free in the morning." Mrs. Pettipiece looked at Rose. "Rose and I could go there first thing."

Rose said, grinning, "Yes, ma'am we can go first thing tomorrow morning." Her head was so light, Rose thought she would faint. She anchored herself in the seat with both feet planted on the floor. She wanted to pinch Cynthia, but she wasn't close enough, so she pinched herself. *Yes, it's real.*

When the realization of what was occurring hit her, Rose leaped out of her seat and hugged Mrs. Pettipiece, and they stood in one joyous embrace. "Thank you, thank you Mrs. P."

"I thank you too, Rose, because of you, my husband has hope for a few more years."

Rose never slept that night, too excited for the future, seeing her children again, providing for them, and giving them the best life possible. Rose wouldn't call her family that night, she would wait until she had the application in her hand, which was only a day or two away. She just continued to give God thanks for what was to come. When negative thoughts of it being a dream, or that Mrs. Pettipiece had changed her mind, crept in, Rose stood firmly on the Word of God, and said, "Get thee behind me Satan!"

The next morning couldn't have come soon enough. Rose, unable to contain her feelings, called her family. She gave them the good news of what was about to transpire in their lives. The screams were so loud Rose was sure everyone on Summerfield Road must have heard the cheers of four very happy children.

Cynthia came to stay with her old friend and neighbour so his wife could go with Rose to begin her legal journey in Canada. Cynthia hugged Rose, and they held each other's hand and said a quiet prayer. She wished Rose and Mrs. Pettipiece well, and saw them off. "You have all your necessary documents, Mrs. P.?"

"It's all here my dear." Mrs. Pettipiece held up the big manila envelope for Cynthia and Rose to see. Rose had given Mrs. Pettipiece the only two IDs she had, which were her passport and birth paper.

Cynthia watched Mrs. Pettipiece drive off with Rose in the passenger seat. She closed the gate behind them and said, "Thank you Lord."

Rose was sharply dressed in one of the dresses she had made but had never got the chance to wear in Canada. She stepped confidently next to Mrs. Pettipiece going into the building. The immigration office was not crowded that early in the morning and Rose counted her blessings. The security guard instructed them to take a number and a seat. Eight people were ahead of them and they waited close to forty minutes to be called. That forty minutes were the longest minutes Rose had ever had to endure. Finally, when her number nine was called, she was hopeful with a nervous stomach. She kept a pleasant face as she walked with Mrs. Pettipiece into the office and took a seat in front of the immigration officer, remembering her "good morning" and "nods" and "smiles". The light headedness and fainting feeling came on, and everything was a blur from then on.

She saw the interaction between Mrs. Pettipiece and the female officer; mouths moving, papers exchanging, but the words were oblivious. When Mrs. Pettipiece nudged her to come, it was time to go, it was as if she was shaken from a trance. "Yes, ma'am."

She grabbed her purse from her lap, turned and smiled with the officer and followed Mrs. Pettipiece out the door. Mrs. Pettipiece didn't wait until they went to the car, she held up the envelope again, and said, "We did it Rose." Rose squeezed Mrs. Pettipiece's hand, her heart was beating so fast. "The hardest part is over," she said, with an equally big grin to Rose's. Rose wanted to hug Mrs. Pettipiece on the steps of the immigration building, but she restrained her overflowing joy until she got home.

No words were needed when she laid eyes on Cynthia waiting on the veranda. They hugged and cried. Rose then hurried to the phone, sure that her anxious family was waiting. Mari picked up the receiver and repeated loudly so all the children, who didn't go to school, too filled with angst, could hear. "Yes, my papers in process!"

"Yes, Mommy, yes!" the children screamed.

"Bless God. Thank you, Jesus," was all Mari could say through her tears.

Michelle Thompson

"It's okay, Mama, God is good," Rose said quietly, through overdue tears of joy.

www.ingramcontent.com/pod-product-compliance
Lightning Source LLC
Jackson TN
JSHW060014160125
76764JS00018B/15